Waking the Sleeping Giant

Peter Wright

BY THE SAME AUTHOR:

Ribbon of Wildness – *Discovering the Watershed of Scotland*, pub: 2010.

Walking with Wildness – *Experiencing the Watershed of Scotland*, pub: 2012.

Nature's Peace – *A Celebration of Scotland's Watershed*, pub: 2013:

Wrights' Roots – *A Comprehensive Family History* (private pub): 2015

DEDICATION

To JMW for her patience and unfailing support

First Published 2017

Published by:

Ribbon *of* Wildness
To start your own journey of discovery..

Copyright © Peter Wright

All rights reserved. No part of this publication may be reproduced, stored, or transmitted in any form, or by any means, electronic, mechanical or otherwise, without the express written permission of the author.

ISBN: 978-0-244-62104-9

Cover photograph by Peter Wright and processed by Thomas Brown

Typeset: main text 11-point Garamond

BIOGRAPHY

Having left school at the age of fourteen, Peter Wright got his first job as a labourer in a chicken hatchery. This was followed by a year of Liberal Studies at Newbattle Abbey College, which he describes as `life changing`. Embarking on a career in youth work, he went on to become Manager of the Duke of Edinburgh`s Award Unit in the City of Edinburgh; a post he held for over twenty years, and during which time, he was awarded MBE.

With his mantra `volunteering makes the world go around`, Peter has been an exemplar of this throughout adult life. From this, a diverse range of organisations have been founded and developed by him, including projects and programmes for children and young people, in heritage, and environmental action.

Writing was an accidental outcome of his epic 1,200 Km walk along the entire Watershed of Scotland when he was in his late fifties, and he has been glad to share his experiences of this with ever-widening public audiences. `Clearly you are having a love-affair . . . with the landscapes of Scotland`, was a perceptive comment by one of his editors, and he is known to be more than happy with this accolade

Chapter One

The phone disintegrated when I slammed it down.

Standing up in a surge of impulsive rage, the desk shook so abruptly that the tankard of pens and pencils overturned; its contents scattering all over the floor. That mug of coffee I`d just made followed suit, pouring liquid all over the keyboard, which immediately erupted in sparks and smoke; the tipping point, in pyrotechnics.

"Fuck sake, that does it I`m out of here for good, had more than enough of this miserable outfit." Eighteen years of commitment to the job, and then some wee office laddie tells me over the phone, that `he regrets I was unsuccessful in my application` - for my job that I`d had to bloody well re-apply for. "It all stinks. Utterly stinks; the tipping point has tipped."

My words bounced around the otherwise empty office.

Grabbing my bag, and cramming a few papers in, I shoved all the rest into the bin. One thing I took some care over, however, was removing my dream-map from the wall, and folded it up neatly; a map of Scotland`s Wild Land Areas.

Stomping through the building, I shouted: "stuff the job, stuff the organisation, no more work with young offenders for me, I`m out of here." With that, I slammed the back door so hard that the big panel of glass shattered, sending shards streaming along the corridor behind. Faces appeared at the rear windows, gaping in astonishment at mild-mannered Andy`s uncharacteristic outburst and trail of destruction; professional persona could be deceptive, though. Unlocking my bike in a swift gesture of disgust; I departed.

Gasping in anger, and for a strong coffee in equal measure, I was off up the road and across Princes Street, where a shiny new Edinburgh tram had to do an emergency stop. The side of this machine close-up and in high-res was not a pretty sight, as I bounced off it, sprawled all over the road, while my bike did a backward cartwheel. But I wasn't stopping for anything. Much bell ringing and I presumed fist-shaking by the driver, seemed to pursue me along to the bridge over the station. Catching half an announcement wafting sky-wards about the `next train to Inverness and all places beyond`, my desperate escape continued towards the Story Telling Centre and that urgently needed coffee.

Sitting at our usual window seat was my trusted, long-standing friend, Ronald, staring idly across the road at The World's End pub. "Christ, you look like you've been attacked by a badger, Andy. What's up pal? Sit down before you fall down; coffee's on its way."

"Just packed in my job, my career, and nearly my life too in an encounter with a tram.

"OK, sit down, calm down, and let's hear about it. The tram didn't win, clearly".

Coffee and a bun arrived; they didn't last long - either of them.

"So, what's the story, Andy"?

"Those bastards in the outfit just informed me that I'd failed in the bid for my job, for fuck sake. Been doing it fine for years, and the office laddie somewhere down there in HQ tells me over the phone, yes, over the bloody phone, that he regrets I've been unsuccessful. How utterly crap is that? Yon` insufferable creep Mike, my former boss, will have been behind it no doubt".

"Did you say you'd packed in your career too"?

With that, my phone rang. "It's the bloody office. They can all go to hell." I angrily switched it off. "Yes, in the time it took me to get here, and not get wiped out by that tram, I decided I've had enough of it. Heading for the hills, that's what I'm going to do right now, or just as soon as I've got a few things together.

"Jesus, that was a bit rash, my friend. You might just regret it."

"Nae` chance. Career is history. Fuck I'd better put in my resignation, though; now. Can you get us another coffee Ronald, and I'll do that? Then I want to ask a real favour of you."

"Sure, but are you certain this is the right thing to do? Have you spoken to Liz, does she know?"

"Not yet. And is it the right course of action? Too true; it's the only thing to do."

As Ronald organised another coffee fix for both of us, I emailed my resignation with immediate effect. Meantime a tour bus full of Japanese tourists was stopped at the traffic lights, and I could see they were all frantically taking photos of that famous pub, The World`s End.

A student mountaineering club had brought us together in an enduring friendship which became mutually beneficial. While I listened to his frustrations in working for one of the National papers, and the subsequent tensions of going freelance, Ronald endured my rantings about local government bureaucracy. Days out on the hill together gave us a shared and quite uncompetitive environmental experience.

When he came back, I asked if I could borrow a tent, sleeping bag, stove, and a few other bits of gear. "I'll need to buy a new pair of boots and waterproofs. The weather might just be OK. It is mid-April. Here`s hoping."

"For you Andy, yes. Anyone else, no chance; as I don't lend my gear."

"Great, thanks. Could you nip home and get it all right now? I'll go up to that shop in Rose Street, and get a couple of things pronto."

"Holy God man, you're in a great steaming hurry."

"Too bloody true. Meet you at the station in about three-quarters of an hour."

"You'll need a rucksack to carry things in."

"Oh, yes, not thinking too straight. Ta."

With that, we were off in our different directions. Going through the station on the way, I padlocked my bike as near to the platform my train would leave from as possible. A rickety looking thing it is, but in this desperate situation, it would just have to do.

Mid-range boots, socks, trousers, tops, waterproofs, gloves, and some expensive dried food, all carried in a frantic hurry out of the shop, with a puzzled looking shop assistant staring after my trail of urgency. Hole-in-the-wall machine in the station for a withdrawal of a few hundred quid and a universal phone charger from the shop saw me heading for a ticket machine. At which, Ronald arrived out of breath.

"Think I've got you all you'll need Andy" As he handed over the rucksack. How the hell are you going cycle with that brute on your back?"

"Necessity, my friend. Right, train's in about five minutes over there. I'm off. Thanks, will let you know where I get to, and when you should get your gear back."

"Eh, good luck, my friend."

With that I was off through the barrier; the divide between my old subservient work life, and an adventurous escapade, the future, perhaps.

With less than a minute to spare before departure, I loaded all my gear and myself onto the train for Inverness and all stations beyond. No going back.

It was only as the train rattled through the girders of the Forth Bridge that it hit home; job, career, and who knows what else, all passing by with iron certainty. Never been out of work in my life, never signed on, been very self-reliant, now at the age of thirty-nine and in otherwise good fettle, the future was a huge question mark. But that uncertainty didn`t dull my conviction that I`d done the right thing, well, for myself, if nothing else. There simply had to be something more than an employer that only seemed to serve its` own narrow introverted purposes masquerading as policies. But I reckoned that my professional life, active environmental interests, political motivations and all the climbing I`d done had kept the lid on any incendiary rebel that might be lurking around within me. The darker things in life, if there were any, lay well hidden.

So, I busied myself in sorting out my gear. Looking across at the bike, I did wonder if it would get me very far; only time would tell. It was as I called it, my town bike, where it remained in Edinburgh for nothing more than getting me around town. Back in Peebles, there was a lovely high-spec well-utilised mountain bike, along with all my other outdoor gear, but on this occasion, needs must. Anyway, where am I heading for, as the only clue so far had been that announcement in the station; to Inverness and whatever, beyond? That`s open-ended, for any great escape.

If anyone studied my demeanour carefully right now, they'd see a man a bit ill at ease with himself. Yes, I could dish out the advice and try at least to sort out a crisis in other people's lives; that's what I'd trained for after all, but a crisis in my life is another matter. And rightly or wrongly, I'd just responded in a way that had created massive uncertainty at the very least. To blame circumstance carried niggling doubts about the wisdom of my actions.

And what of Liz, and our well established, if the slightly unusual relationship or living arrangements? Was I fair to her? Would my actions and what they implied about attitudes, betray the trust and affection we had built together over five or more years? The meandering lines of a passing river course betokened neither purpose nor direction. Entering a tunnel, with the sudden change of sound and light jolted me out of my self-doubt.

Someone had mentioned a place called Rhidorroch to me recently. Said it was a strange, mysterious, beautiful place, and that they were sure I'd just love to explore it. That'll do nicely, but where the fuck is it? Looking around the carriage, I found a railway network map, and study it as I might, could find no sign of this elusive Rhidorroch place. Ah, then I did remember one wee snippet about it, my informant said it was a bit north of Ullapool. Oh fuck, that's on the west coast, and this train is heading up the east side of the country.

Nothing for it then, but a bumpy cycle ride from one side of Scotland to the other.

Going back to the rail map, it looked like the nearest station was Ardgay, some way north of Inverness. I'd get a local map when I changed trains there.

As the train glided through the trees above the gorge, and past the site of the Battle of Killiecrankie, reckoned I'd be best to phone Liz and explain.

"You've done what?" She gasped in utter disbelief, at the other end. "Must have taken leave of your senses, Andy."

"Well I didn't get the job, the bastards have given my post to someone else. Been doing the job fine, and that's what the outfit's policy, if you can call it that, does to you, so I've jacked in the whole insufferable thing."

Silence.

"And I'm on the train north, heading for the hills, got to clear my head a bit."

"You mean, what you're doing is you are just escaping, doing a bunk, from all of your responsibilities. You bastard, hey, what about me, where do I fit into your bloody plans, the very least you could've done was talk it over with me, before just buggering off like this. And where did you say you are going anyway?"

"Didn't say, but I'm going to an area called Rhidorroch for a few days. Just to get my brain back together."

"Rhid, where? You might end up leaving your wits there. And yourself as well come to think of it."

"Rhidorroch, it's just north of Ullapool. Someone told me it's an exciting and mysterious kind of place that I should explore. Am strangely drawn to it, like something is calling me there."

"Well, there's no mystery to this. How's about you explore your common sense? Career and pension, security, and income; all out of the window in one fit of pique, just because you didn't get that job. Yes, I'm sorry about that, your boss Mike is a complete pillock, we know that, but I didn't think you were too. Now I'm beginning to wonder."

"Hey, I'll be back in a few days I reckon, Liz. Why so angry?"

"Because you've just demonstrated an utterly selfish side of your character that I don't recognise, 'till now that is. How could you? We've always done things and planned the big events together, and with our domestic arrangements; always agreed that it's the way we both want it, that it suits us. Now you go and throw something as big as this right up in the air, without involving me at all. You are a selfish bastard, Andy Borthwick. There's Sunday lunch coming up at Hermione and Jamie's; then there's my cousin Charles' wedding at Mar Lodge. And are you remembering that you promised, you promised, absolutely promised, to help me with my Fringe Exhibition this summer. There's one hell of a lot a lot at stake here, and you've just mucked it, fucked it all up, Andy."

"Good God Liz, I'm only going to be away for a few days, then we'll be back to normal, I promise."

"Oh, no we won't, because by doing what you've done, and the way you're going about it, you've broken something between us. In fact, when, if you do get back, just bugger off back to your flat in Peebles, I'm not sure when or if I'll want to see you again."

"But Liz. " She'd hung up. In desperation, I tried phoning again and again, on both her land-line and mobile. No response.

I'd fucked things up for sure, or so it seemed, but was still resolutely intent on getting The Outfit and its bureaucratic miasma right out of my head, right out of my system altogether. Only one way to do that, and that's to get out among the hills.

Need to try and sort things out with Liz when I do get back, though, I told myself optimistically.

The harsh realities of my great escape hit me during the couple of hours I had between trains in Inverness; acting rashly at the time may have had its appeal, but the urgency of getting food for three or more days out in the wilds was pressing. The same confusion about the adequacy of my kit and clothing for mid-April conditions, all buzzed around in my head. Instinct kicked in, though, as I swept from the supermarket to outdoors and cycle shops in a mad helter-skelter, with my last port of call being the shop in the station. There I grabbed a couple of bars of chocolate for the rest of the journey, and a book with a title that somehow caught my eye: `Folk Traditions and Faery Beings in Scotland's Wild Places: The Highlands`.

At least I'd have an hour or more on the train to repack properly. My phone rang in amongst all this, and I could see it was Liz, but decided to ignore the call for now; I was on a mission to unclutter my brain after the morning's trauma.

While looking nervously across at my town bike, there seemed to be doubt about whether it would survive a coast-to-coast on the tracks I'd rashly chosen as a route into the wilder west.

Chapter Two

Extricating myself, bike, and gear from the train in Ardgay, I could see that the light was beginning to fade into a glorious pink sky. With only a head torch, there was a limit to how far I could get before dark, though, so I camped just a few miles up the valley. Sleep there should have been calm and sweet, as the sound of a nearby burn provided the night music, but it was discordant as my mind was all over the place. Although I'd have the conviction of knowing that my decision to jack-in my career was the right thing, it now carried with it niggling thoughts about what next? That conversation with Liz had put me into confusion; I may need to get away to re-charge right now, but what sort of a reception might I get on my return to Edinburgh in a few days? Things that had all seemed so settled just twenty-four hours earlier were now in a state of flux.

Oh, I liked the contrast between my part-time rural life in Peebles with river bank and hill so close at hand. There was a sense of community around me that only in hindsight I saw mirrored my Galloway upbringing on the one hand, and the buzz of the City with Liz and a professional life in Edinburgh, on the other. Liz had often commented that it suited her too in giving her space and time she needed for her creative talents to grow. We knew we had each other, and respected our personal traits. But what now? It was a long and troubled night.

By mid-afternoon the following day, however, I finally arrived in Rhidorroch, exhausted.

In no state to start exploring despite the snippets of enticing information I'd had about the area, I set up camp beside a lochan in the middle of a full amphitheatre of moor, lochs, and hollows surrounded by a ring of small ragged hills.

Reading the first couple of chapters of my book compellingly drew me into the other-world possibilities of this place, where I found myself oddly yet calmly embracing notions that the purely rational is somehow on hold, to allow a deeper, more profound dimension to my very being.

Sleep was, at last, real, and peaceful.

The whole day which followed was spent exploring much of the area. Here I discovered that it extended to many square miles of utterly randomly shaped lochs and rough moorland dressed in the remains of the previous season's heather and bog myrtle. Crags and high rocks stranded among the surrounding sea of treeless vegetation in every hue of brown, grey, and yellow through to white; in a subtle and immensely varied palette. There seemed to be no pattern to the flow of this landscape; whatever had formed it appeared to have lacked any apparent plan. Contours marked on the map looked like they'd been blown this way and that before the ink had dried in random squiggles. The previous description of strange, mysterious, and beautiful seemed just right, and I was beginning to feel captivated by this delightful place. Was it fate perhaps that had been directing someone to tell me a little about it so recently; just enough to arouse my curiosity?

The sky had clouded over by dusk, and a breeze crept in from the west.

Slowly drifting off to sleep, I was leaving so much behind. A career that had ceased to satisfy. An employer that for whatever reason, failed to show any regard for its employees, and an organisational machine that was devoid of purpose, other than its inward looking one. My thoughts turned to Liz, and of both her anger and concern. Memories strayed back to my upbringing in Galloway, for this was where my love of hillwalking, camping or staying overnight in a bothy had first been experienced. There, the seeds of my grave environmental concerns were first sown and took root. Liz and I now shared these passions together, for, in addition to the Scottish mountain areas which we so enjoyed, we'd splashed out twice on trips to the Pyrenees and Tatras. Very memorable experiences these had been. Whether we would ever venture again to these or any other foreign challenges, only time would tell. Wondering whether we'd do anything together ever again raced through my mental turmoil.

So, in half sleeping, these, and so many other awareness's drifted in and out of a very blurred kind of focus.

Sometime in the middle of the night, I awoke suddenly, for it became evident that the weather had changed dramatically. Not only was it raining heavily, drumming loudly on Ronald's frail tent, but the wind had got up; with a vengeance. Gathering my wits about me as fast as possible, to take some stock of the situation, and donning my head torch, I wondered first, if there was any gear still outside, which might be lost. Thankfully reassuring myself on that count as everything had been well stored, I then considered the site I'd chosen, pondering whether it would remain safe from flooding, or passing missiles in the form of airborne debris. Again, I satisfied myself that I'd chosen wisely. Finally, had I erected and pegged the tent to as near perfection as could be, but remembered checking and re-checking all the pegs, guys, and the orientation. Doubted if any better result could have been accomplished.

Turning my attention to the inside of the tent, I shone the torch on the fabric and poles. If there was any sleep left in me, it was gone; shattered in an instant. The poles were bending, flexing, and willowing in a mad wind-wrenched frenzy. The sides would belly-in from the left almost touching me, and just as soon pull away with that same threatening movement coming at me on the right side. The apex, or what there was of it, dipped and dived in a hysteria of lurching madness. The fabric could only hold this onslaught from without, in the tension between the poles. Realising that I`d never experienced anything so dramatic before, it was evident that this was new testing; courage needed.

Switching the light off, I just lay there in the black and noise, and waited. It was like being beside a large steam engine. Nothing could be done to improve the situation, I was at its mercy, utterly. Through the hours that passed, all sorts of disturbing thoughts about potential loss or destruction of my gear, and indeed of my safety, swooped-in relentlessly. Wild camping could be just that, and it was proving to be so this night. In the wide-open expanses of the natural environment, where the elements would have their way, the pod that I was in, was gossamer thin. Only the art and engineering of good tent design could ease my predicament. A string of what-iffs raced through my mind, and all were unresolved. With every assault on the tent, I felt frail and insignificant.

Perhaps out of despair, or an overdose of irrational thoughts, I must have finally drifted back to sleep; it was fitful. The dark watches can be a fearful place, where reality is within as ephemeral a boundary as the tent itself. Some sleep at least must eventually have taken a fragile hold.

In the calmer new day, I could see that beyond the immediate area of upland, the land fell away to the west, towards a valley and the sea somewhere beyond. Areas of sea loch were interrupted by islands and yet more of the mainland. Mountains seemed to rear assertively, grandly even, out of the sea or moorland. It would have been easy to become quite bewitched by it all, as a very light breeze drifted across the landscape, softly caught my hair, caressed it, and moved on. Puffy clouds sailed slowly across an otherwise clear blue sky. Any lingering cares drifted away too, for the time being, at least.

Dropping slowly down into one of the many hollows and edging my way around all the lush green erupting knee-high moss-domes, I stood with a sense of charmed delight at the soothing calm that seemed to fill the air here. Slowly adjusting to the very different atmosphere and the real sense of peace, that touched me deeply, and looking over towards a crag that formed the southern boundary of this strange and beautiful place, I became aware of a mysterious looking figure. Perhaps looking across at me, or in my direction at least; he moved slowly towards me, beckoning in a slow, unhurried movement of the arm.

He was quite unlike anything or anyone I'd ever met. His tanned and deeply wrinkled face looked ancient, with small narrow all-seeing eyes. His weathered cloak almost brushed the ground, and it had a hood that only showed the front of his kindly face. With sagging shoulders or just the way the cloak hung so loosely on him, there was no discernible individual shape within, as it ran in a simple sweep from hood to ground cover. This great cloak was the same spectrum of natural palette as the vegetation surrounding where we stood. It was as if I was somehow under his spell, and that there was perhaps some sympathy or bond between us.

"Hello, this is a lovely and mystical sort of place, isn't it?" I ventured.

He nodded towards a large flat rock near the base of the crag. Responding to the gesture, we sat down together.

"Yes, it's all that, and so much more. Welcome, and what brings you to these parts?"

Deciding not to bother him with all the work nonsense, which would have seemed so very out of place in his mossy enclosure, I just replied that I was seeking a few of days of peace to discover more of this delightful area and to find more of myself perhaps too.

"Ah, you may well have come to the right place," he said in his quiet light confident voice.

I could make nothing of any accent he may have had, and it seemed irrelevant to pursue that thought further.

"Do you live hereabouts", I asked, looking around for a shack or shelter of any kind?

"Yes, and I can imagine what it is you are looking for. I`ve no ordinary abode but find my refuge and protection among the rocks, mosses, and myrtle banks. I`m of this place, and it of me; have been for more years than I care to count. What little food I need, I find around me, and have the ancient wisdom of knowing what is safe and sweet."

He was venturing quite a lot about himself to me, a perfect stranger. While I found this unusual, here and from him it somehow just felt quite natural. For this was his landscape, and I, a rare visitor; he could choose to whom he might want to make himself known. His cloak was a perfect camouflage in which to blend into his surroundings, if he so chose.

We talked about many different things over the next couple of hours. It was a natural, easy conversation, and I could sense that he was skilfully steering our discussion along to his agenda. Despite his apparent remoteness from life in the wider community, he was none-the-less surprisingly well informed on contemporary and deeper environmental issues. Where he obtained his information, I couldn`t imagine, but as we talked, I found we agreed on so many things to do with the natural world in Scotland today, so he was most certainly not in any way isolated or inward looking. He had the pressing matters of debate and urgency for real land-reform well assembled in his mind and could express them clearly, albeit in his distinctive way. He saw the different tensions in land-use, ownership, the place of people in it, conservation, the pursuit of differing interests both good and bad. I just felt that he was giving me a mature and well-argued lesson on how things should be, on how they must go as if we saw beyond the present.

As he appeared to tire somewhat, I readied myself for the nub of what he might be seeking, what he yearned for, and perhaps even of my likely part in it.

"Over my lifetime, I've accumulated a lot of knowledge about our wilder landscapes, and of the many influences that have had a bearing on them, for good or ill, over extended periods of time. Somehow, I've found myself able to look deeper than most, into the very soul of the terrain we cherish and which nourishes our spirit, if we care or even dare to let it. There is much in it which could give cause for despair of course, for we are not especially good stewards. Partisan interests, politics and sheer inertia are our chief foes, inhibiting change for the good that I crave. It's certainly not lack of knowledge that holds us back; we have plenty of that. How to use it wisely, how to harness the wisdom in it is the challenge."

Listening intently to his every word, it was clear that I'd met someone with a profound natural insight.

"Do go on, please; I'm in no hurry."

"Thank you for listening, and for hearing. Whether I am nearing the end of my journey, I've no real way of knowing. But if the knowledge and understanding that I have is to be of any benefit,

I have known for some time, that I need to bring it together into something simple but comprehensive for us here in Scotland; something timeless."

"That would be an immense challenge for anyone to do, as there are so many opinions, ideas, theories, and differing interests to contend with in all this," I ventured cautiously. "Believe me, I`ve read, debated, and discussed many of them, at some length."

"Yes, I imagined that you would have. In I sense, I was in no desperate hurry to crystallise my thoughts and values, because seeking out the soul of the landscape is beyond the normal parameters of time or the human span. But therein must lie the simple formula that is the right one. The one big thing that gets in the way of much of it is human pride of course, in all its forms; our environmental arrogance, indeed."

He paused in the silence, to focus clearly on his mission. Patience came easily, though.

Looking up slowly and scanning all that was around us, he continued, but with perhaps more caution this time. "In all my thinking and collected knowledge, and more importantly my atunement to my surroundings, our environment, I`ve narrowed my attentions to one unique landscape or geographic feature. It is one which runs the entire length of the country, and was created in the almost immeasurable time span of Nature herself; by Nature, alone. It's a very simple one, visible, and characterises the best, the most comprehensive and mostly continuous wildness that we`ve inherited today, or are ever likely to have now. I would go so far as to say that it is quite simply an artery of Nature, one that runs the entire length of Scotland. Indeed, if we will but let it, many of our best wilder landscapes are united by it."

The effort and concentration needed in telling me this was by now sapping his energy, so I acknowledged this by saying: "you look tired, and it's very clear you care more about this than anything else on earth. If you would like a rest, I can come back later."

"Thank you, but I'll continue, as I've almost finished, for now at any rate. You are the one that I sought to call to this place, to engage with about my passions and deep concerns. I'm going to entrust something to you, and just hope that my faith in you to do something positive and to last with is sound. I believe that in you, I have chosen well, as I've observed you exploring the area, your apparent understanding of it, and I think discovering the essence of this place. The signs must have brought you to me. Please take what I'm about to give into your care, and use it wisely. You will find it has the power to give a new entirely positive perspective on our countryside, and on how it may be nurtured in the future. Its implications and potential are truly immense for people and communities. I was never one for causes or organisations, hence my minimal living here with Nature as my companion, in the richest and deepest eco-spiritual life imaginable."

"But what are you going to entrust me with?" I asked with a little impatience. He gave no answer.

He then did something quite remarkable, in gesturing silently and drawing my attention away to one crag, with a buzzard soaring effortlessly high overhead, I found that I was strangely focussed on it, and not on him. When I looked around, he was gone, back into the landscape he loved. Where he had been sitting lay a small piece of ancient looking paper folded with real and deliberate care. Written on the outside were the simple words, `The Seven Signs`.

Picking it up gently, and opening the fragile document, I read slowly: `The Seven Signs of Enduring and Continuous Wildness`. These were then listed:

1. Upon the elevated lands above the waterheads

2. In landscapes formed over time by Nature alone

3. Cresting a myriad of tops and rocky crags

4. Embracing irreplaceable deep peat and flow

5. Where diverse habitats span the least cultivated along those empty ridges

6. Imbued with folklore and rich in symbolism

7. Our native artery of inspiration for the Human Spirit

Reading it repeatedly, I tried to make sense of this very succinct eco-missal. Every word must have been very well chosen I imagined, and the simple, comprehensive nature of it applicable in some way to much of Scotland.

Looking once more at the spot where my companion had been sitting so briefly, I realised that this scrap of paper might hold the answer to what I might explore in the foreseeable future; I had a quest and responsibility too.

As a precaution, given how fragile the paper appeared to be, I typed the text into my smartphone. Then, I emailed it to myself; feeling a real sense of reverence for it in the process.

On returning to my tent, a brew-up and snack were called for, as I methodically packed up all my gear, and added a few more photos to the growing collection in my camera. Somehow, this digital gallery had already acquired a title, in my head at least: Lands and Spirit of Rhidorroch.

With just four hours of good daylight left, I reckoned on time enough to get back out to Ullapool before dark, and would head home the following day all being well. So before leaving the higher ground, I texted Liz with my plans, hoping that by now she'd have calmed down a bit, and perhaps even be pleased to see me, in due course. First, I'd to retrieve my bike from where it was safely hidden among rafters in the loch boat-house a couple of days earlier. To get there, it was a relatively easy undulating walk along the top of a line of almost vertical crags, from where I looked down hundreds of feet to the valley bottom below. From this vantage, I pondered the strange and beautiful area I'd discovered and the character that I now called The Spirit, that I'd met here. His Seven Signs seemed to be quite incomprehensible and would take an imaginative investigation to unravel. He had given me a quest, a mission to pursue, and this more than anything had cleared my head; giving a purposeful feeling that I was ready for the next chapter. Strange, I thought, how quickly things can change from anger and confusion to a new and apparently worthwhile direction - even if the focus was still quite unclear.

But I knew I had to keep a sense of perspective on things, as the biggest unknown at present was the future of the relationship between Liz and myself. Though confident that I wished it to continue and grow, I honestly hadn't been prepared for the strength of her apparent dismay with what I'd done in packing in a safe career and the way I'd gone about it. She liked order in her life, and this had thrown it into disarray. We'd been together for over five years, and our semi-detached fulfilment, as she put it, didn't cloud our relationship. Rather, it suited both of our lifestyles, which each respected in the other. She lived in Edinburgh all the time, and I lived in my flat in Peebles some of the time; we were together when it suited mutually. Her work in the Fine Art department at the University paid her bills and left time for a greater interest in landscape photography and poetry. There was much in her talents and vision that I admired greatly.

My thoughts also turned to Ronald, and our shared passions for high wild places, the landform of Scotland, and what he called `the compelling place of people` in all of it. Having met years ago, through a student mountaineering club, we had continued to enjoy mountain outings together. Philosophy had been his subject, and I found that he used it well both as a freelance journalist in the outdoor and ecological themes, but also in developing the political and social imperatives for land reform. It was hard not to be drawn into the causes he cherished, and his ability to write lucidly about them. That we would work together on my embryonic mission seemed likely.

Meantime, though, my vantage from the top of these crags appeared to cover both the most recent experiences in the wildness of this area and the wider aspects of my life. The severe drop which loomed to my right suggested a precariousness of the path that I must tread.

Arriving in Ullapool in the dark, I found a hostel, which was thankfully not busy, and enjoyed the pleasures of a shower, and at least a partial change of clothes. A meal and a pint in the Ceilidh Place completed the sense of return to more comfortable domestic indulgence.

Chapter Three

If those brief couple of days in the wilds of Rhidorroch had succeeded in giving me new direction and purpose, they'd also raised my level of anxiety about Liz and myself. The journey south was not as relaxed and optimistic as anticipated.

When I'd phoned her later the previous evening, our conversation had been tense. Having shown interest in what she had been doing while I'd been away, her replies to my questions were terse, while my enthusiasm about my experiences met with much the same uncharacteristically tepid response.

Something had changed. Try as I might, there seemed to be no way of steering the conversation towards a more active interest.

"I may have calmed down Andy, but I'm still deeply hurt with your ill-thought-out impulsive actions and the way in which you excluded me from playing any part in them. I'd have expected much better of you. How could you do it? I mean, didn't you just pause for a brief minute or two to consider what you were doing, and perhaps you should be less selfish? Did you honestly think it all through properly? My language may be more temperate than when we spoke on Monday, but do not be deceived, don't think you can just waltz back down the road, and pick up where we left off. I'm simply not having it. You've behaved towards me like a real prat."

This reaction was both the Liz I knew and thought I loved, but it was also a stranger. Yes, she liked to be organised and settled and to know where she stood. She wanted everything in her life to be in its place, in order. But I was still taken aback, by this reaction of hers, to my need to get away for a few days, and to her dismay at the fact that I'd packed in my career. Was it worth that much, anyway?

"Liz, I'm on the train right now, so having this rather public conversation is, well, a bit open. Can we get together this evening, and talk things over? I still love you, and I want you to hear that I want you to know it. But surely the best thing we can do is at least to have a decent chat with no audience?"

"I don't know; I've plans to go to a talk at the National Library. Why should I change these plans just to suit you?"

"Because I'm asking you, please, to do me the courtesy at least, of hearing my side of things, and to see how we can work this out, together."

"What time does your train get in, when will you be back in Edinburgh?"

"I'll be in by half-four, Liz."

Much against my better judgment, I'll meet you for a coffee in the Library at around five. Are you respectable?"

"Yes, reasonably so, I was in a good wee hostel last night. Thank you, Liz, I appreciate this. I just hope .."

"Well don't hope for too much, Andy."

Although the cafe was busy, we did find a table at the back, almost behind the stairs.

"Before we even start, I'm wondering do you realise just why I'm so pissed-off with you?"

"I most certainly do now, Liz. And I'm truly sorry that this has caused so much difficulty for us."

"No doubt you are sorry, but I just do not like being disregarded, and in the way, you've done this. Ditching your career on a whim, and then just informing me that you're on your way to the hills, or wherever it was, without even doing the decent thing, and talking it all over with me first, is not on. Bloody hell, we've been together in our way for five years now, and you just pack in the safe and secure, and hit the road. That's what I can't understand, and feel deeply let down by you for it."

The conversation continued in this way for some time. Well, more of an interrogation. I was very much on the spot, a position I wasn't used to, well not with Liz at any rate. Doing my very best to convince her that my decision about work was the right one, I did acknowledge that I could have done it all a bit differently; but this seemed to make little difference. She was angry and hurt, and wouldn't let go of that easily. Piling on the apologies, and reassurances that this had been a highly provoked one-off, and would not be repeated, only blunted the cut of her rage ever so slightly. But I persevered.

With hunger beginning to get to me, and the imminent prospect of closing time, I cautiously suggested food.

"I'll hand it to you, Andy, you don't give up easily; you are a persistent bugger. I'd feared that our meeting up like this would mellow my resolve to call it a day. And I've missed that talk that I was going to go to in the hall over there. Talk about disruption, well you've done that all right. You'll have some difficulty getting back to Peebles at this hour tonight with your bike. There's some food in the house, and be clear about one thing, you are on the settee. This impasse is unfinished business. Don't read anything into the gesture."

The conversation continued, but in a less aggressive tone on Liz's part, as we ate an omelette at her kitchen table. Broken eggs and omelettes seemed to kind of sum up where we were.

"Can we talk this through tomorrow Liz, I want to resolve the damage I've clearly done?"

"Yes, suppose so, I've no commitments till the afternoon. Meantime, so that we can at least be civilised about things, tell me briefly, what you've been up to in Rhid, Rhidorroch? Where did you say, it is, never heard of it?"

Without overdoing the real need for me to clear my head by escaping to the hills, I focussed more on the exploration of a wild, intriguing, and beautiful area, and what a revelation it had been. "It's north of Ullapool, you may remember it better from when we climbed some of the mountains a bit east of it a couple of years ago, but we'd approached it from the east."

"Oh yes, I do remember the great views that we had, out over the sea to the western isles from one of the tops. Seana something you said it was."

"Yes, Seana Bhraigh, quite a favourite amongst Munroists it is. Rhidorroch is kind of between there and the coastlands. So, I spent a whole day exploring it in a meandering kind of way. That night, I thought my end had come, as there was a hoolie of a storm. Thought the tent would disintegrate, and me inside it. Thankfully it and I survived. Next day, I met this strange, almost mystical character, who talked at length in a very moving way about the environment, conservation, land reform and a whole lot more. He has entrusted to me what he has called The Seven Signs of Enduring and Continuous Wildness, and hopes I, we, can do something with this eco-missal."

"Oh, can we now? No, tell me what these seven signs are first." Curiosity had, at last, got the better of her.

We talked at some length about them, and hadn't unravelled the conundrum when Liz said: "Right, I'm knackered, so you know where the settee is, you'll have your sleeping bag, but there are some of your clothes in the usual place."

Although I was physically comfortable on her large settee in the equally large sitting room, I was still very uncomfortable in every other respect and slept poorly. My great escape carried grim consequences for me.

Would I have done things any differently, I did wonder, as I had a shower before breakfast? That bloody curate's egg again - good in places. No intention whatever of recanting on my actions regarding The Outfit and whatever job may have been waiting for me by way of compensation. No chance. But I'd clearly made a hash of it in not taking the time and care to talk to Liz first, before fleeing the scene.

"Morning Andy, hope you slept well."

"Perfectly comfortable thanks, but didn't sleep all that well, 'because I know I've made a hash of things, and should have been much more thoughtful about talking with you first, Liz."

"Aha yes, but let's see where things take us. Some breakfast first, what would you like?

"Cereal and coffee will be all right, thanks."

"I'll make us coffee, help yourself to the cereal."

As we sat down at the table, Liz casually mentioned that she'd had a phone conversation with her sister Hermione the other day. She says the girls are, OK but their dad Jamie seems to be behaving a bit odd, she says.

"Oh, in what way?

"Awkwardly intense, were the words she used, and not his usual well, reasonable, if rather formal self. Mind you he likes to make a bit of thing about being respectable. Ach well, he'll get over it. It's Sunday lunch there a week on Sunday. Will you be there?"

"Sure thing, if I`m still invited to it, Liz."

"Well let's see how things shape up between us this morning."

Keeping my feelings on this remark very much to myself, I did think, well there is hope.

"Tell me about this sort of quest that the mysterious spirit character has given you to pursue for him."

Oh fuck, this is dangerous territory, I thought, especially at this stage in the proceedings. Very quick thinking called for here. "I`m honestly not sure what it is, haven`t been able to make any sense of it. It is a conundrum for sure, and until I`ve had a look at some maps, and talked the possible meaning of it all over with Ronald, I don`t know what it adds up to if anything. I`ve arranged to meet him this evening at the Sheraton, why don`t you come along too? I might have made something of the first sign, the one about the lands above the waterheads, by then."

"You seem to be making a big assumption about staying here again tonight" She snapped."

"Oh God, this is all coming out back to front Liz, I`m sorry. Could I please stay here again?"

"I suppose. But don`t be getting any big ideas."

"Thank you, I do appreciate this Liz, especially after the way I`ve treated you. Can I ask one other wee thing?"

"Christ, you do have a cheek, but what is it?

"Can I put some washing in the machine, then we'll talk?"

Gesturing, she poured us some more coffee.

Wasting no time, I grabbed the collection of clothes I'd left in a heap in the sitting room, and had them into the machine, pronto.

"Right, I admit I was a bit harsh in the way I reacted to your news when we spoke on Monday. And hanging up on you was not entirely fair. That said, what you have done, and the way you did it is hard for me to take, and equally hard for me to understand. You do see that, don't you?"

"Eh, yes, it was most unfair, not to say improper of me, and I'm truly sorry Liz. But I'm sure you'll acknowledge that jacking in the job was probably coming anyway, and this was the catalyst for it to happen. I need to make something more exciting of my work life, whatever that turns out to be. I've worked since the day and hour that I left school. Even when I was at Uni`, I worked weekends and holidays. Totally self-reliant. Now I've propelled it into a wee bit of an unknown."

"You sure as hell have, but I do acknowledge that you were no longer getting anything out of that work, regarding personal satisfaction, that is."

"Take this whatever way you feel able Liz after the events of this week, but you mean everything to me, and I'm deeply sorry for the hurt I've caused you. If I could wind the clock back."

"Well, you know you can't do that because what's done is done. Although I find I can't just switch off from you and us, that trust is on a shaky peg. I'm willing, agreeable to trying to work this out if we can Andy, but you'll have to remember just what happens when you go taking me for granted. Now I need to go, but I'll see you at teatime. Not sure what there is to eat, mind you."

As she walked across the Meadows to her work in the older part of the University, Liz`s pace slowed. She ponderous, she wondered at the turmoil that had entered her life so abruptly in the last few days; reasonably established certainties with which she felt so comfortable, had been shaken.

With no lectures or tutorials to deliver that morning, she sat down on a bench in George Square gardens to contemplate. Although unaccustomed to this kind of indulgent use of her time, she briefly took stock of her life and living to-date: school, family, university, work, and relationships, were all given at least a cursory mulling over. But the recent uncertainties meant that it was now all a bit mixed up, and very upsetting. What was she to make of Andy following his impulsive and self-centred actions? Did this threaten their future together, and could she trust him now? Her mind ranged over how they had first met and got together, with all the implications that that bore at the time, and how utterly intrigued she`d been with this very high-spirited young man. He`d turned her life upside down then, and was doing much the same, but in a very different way this time round.

Liz knew that she wanted things she could be sure of, a relationship she could depend upon, but could see that it was on the unsteady ground right now.

Students came and went through the gardens, the dappled sunlight played on young shoots in the trees, and a regular buzz from unseen vehicles nearby subtly reminded her of the patterns and rhythm of life in the City. She knew she was not alone, but for once in her life, felt a bit cut off from its more usual reassurances.

When she'd been looking around for a flat to purchase a few years back, she'd been naturally drawn to the Bruntsfield area with its tall well-ordered and in places flamboyant tenements. Confident Edinburgh in crisp sandstone, harking back to a rich historical provenance but embracing the best design of the times entirely. Liz knew from the outset that it would reflect well her sense of good domestic taste when adapted to comfortable present-day living. She and Andy had often discussed this concession to refinement, as he put it, but they had no wish to alter their modus operandi, none-the-less.

Urban living suited Liz well, and she could go out comfortably from there to indulge her passion for capturing the landscape and wildlife on her camera. Andy preferred semi-rural domestic arrangements some of the time, for a quick getaway to the hills, as he put it.

The sound of raucous laughter nearby brought Liz back to more immediate concerns.

Chapter Four

Sitting down in front of my laptop at the large kitchen table in Liz's flat in Lauderdale Street, I'd pulled together all the information to hand, and spread out a large map of Scotland on the floor, with a highlighter pen at the ready.

The starting point was the 'Seven Signs' that had been given to me so trustingly by he whom I now called The Spirit. This brief missal was tantalising stuff; 'The Seven Signs of Enduring and Continuous Wildness'. 'I Had to assume that every word in it was there, with a purpose and that together they contained all the clues needed to unravel the mystery; a problem-solving exercise on an epic scale. Why had The Spirit chosen me, to do something that he apparently felt was of the utmost importance to the Scotland and her people today? What could there possibly be that was so original and yet untold in environmental realms? And how could it, as he had hinted, have such significance for the human spirit? What would I do with it once the riddle had been solved, I did wonder, as it must be something big; a quest like no other. Reading books could perhaps hold the answer, but which books, and there are so very many of them? No, he had put in my hands just a few phrases that somehow would set the right direction. Everything would hopefully become clearer to me and about me, as I worked my way into it.

Reading yet again, his Seven Signs of Enduring and Continuous Wildness, I decided to concentrate on just the first for now. 'Spectacular lands above the waterheads', what on earth could that mean? Only one thing to do and that was to be clear about the exact meaning of the key words. So, the dictionary was pressed into action, well thumbed, and notes were taken on each, as they were scrutinised in turn. Wikipedia also added further insight, and within an hour or so, I was happy on the meanings and their subtleties. Which of the big waterheads needed to be identified though, and are they in any way linked?

But my eye kept being caught by the last one, perhaps hardest of all, what I was already calling the enrichment of the human spirit; what artery is it that was being described, and on such a scale, would it be of truly major significance? And in Scotland?

Back to the first though with a reminder to myself, I emphasised the words enduring and continuous, if the concept of wildness in all this, was at least clear enough.

The Spirit had given an immense task, but it was one to be relished, and one I earnestly hoped could receive full justice and an abiding outcome.

So, I'd to assume that by waterheads, he meant the sources of streams, and then from that, the river systems that they were all centred on. The rivers of the eastern side of the country seemed like a good start. So, I called up my geographic knowledge about rivers in Scotland and then identified the primary ones on the eastern side of the map: Tweed, Forth, Tay, Dee, Don, Spey, Beauly, Kildonan and so on. The highlighter pen which had been at the ready was rapidly pressed into action, and a small `x` put on the map spread out on the floor, at the source of each of these great rivers. Reminding myself that every river must go somewhere, the destinations of these were noted as being the North Sea; they certainly had that in common.

The same exercise was then followed assiduously for the western rivers, including Ayr, Clyde, Etive, Coe, Garry, and some much shorter Waters further north including Halladale and Thurso, which lay around the corner along the north coast. The highlighter was out once again, and some small `x` marks the spot placed at each source. Although the picture was confused with all those peninsulas, firths, and islands off the west coast, the Atlantic, or something connected directly to it seemed to be a common link for them.

Standing back, I looked at the very unclear picture. What was missing in this, though?

Muttering to myself, time for a coffee break, I shuffled across and got the kettle on, coffee apparatus out, mug on the table, and with biscuit in hand, returned to the quest a few minutes later.

To make real sense of it, it was clear I'd need to focus on the first of the seven signs, as this must be the primary one, providing the key that would perhaps open the first door. It was the `what`, and the others were more descriptive, or about landscape character, quality, and of course some sense of people and spirituality in it all too. So, if the headwaters one could be solved I'd be making good progress, and the others might just follow-on from that. Back to the map then.

It occurred that the one thing that was determining the difference between the two groups of rivers was their destination. It wasn't so much about east and west, but about which body of water they would finally empty into; the North Sea or the Atlantic Ocean; a strikingly simple distinction. So, if that was the case, then everything that wasn't the North Sea in destination, must be Atlantic bound. The North Sea was the smaller and easier to define. So, I looked again at rivers flowing into this, and apart from one significant anomaly they were all clear in their destination. Then my attention was given to the rivers in the southwest and concluded that they were clearly connected to that Ocean via the Irish Sea. I grew excited as I traced the sources of the Esk and Annan. After the relevant `x` marks had been added to the map, I turned my attention to the north, with the Thurso, Halladale, and Naver. Tracing them up from sea to source was straightforward, so more distinctive marks were added to the map.

Standing back, and once again taking a critical look at my efforts, I felt I was onto something, a something that might just enable me to link the `x` marks in some way. From this, I'd work out their significance, and begin to be able to plot it all on the more detailed digital map that I had on my laptop. But what had started as something rather like making a jigsaw that had a few pieces missing, with a few extra pieces added from an entirely different picture thrown in, was nonetheless just beginning to come together.

Some time was then spent looking at smaller rivers to see where they ended up, whether it was in one of the bigger river systems, or flowed directly into the brine on its own. More `x` marks appeared. But I was challenged with the rivers Spey and Tay; both regarding where their sources were, and what flowed into them. They're eastbound, I reasoned, so if I could be sure about a line connecting the Atlantic side, then that might clarify the other.

Tentatively, the highlighter pen moved across the map to get a line that didn't cross any running water; it seemed to start on or around a hill called Peel Fell on the border with England and concluded at Duncansby Head in the north-east. Joining the dots, or the X's to be exact, created the picture.

Time for a late lunch, for this, had been a long exercise, and I was somewhat weary with it. A café just across Bruntsfield Links would give me both the snack and diversion that was needed. `Could return to this, after the break with a clear head, I very much hoped.

On my return, and with a new fund of energy, I went through that oft criticised ritual of opening and starting my laptop; habits die hard. The only email that caught my eye was that one from Ronald asking me if we'd meet up later for a chat about my new venture. From what he was saying albeit briefly, it seemed to have captured his interest too. So, I replied and confirmed we meet in the Sheraton at seven, and that Liz might join us too. It was usually friendly and relaxed, rarely too busy, and a good place for a chat. It was also reasonably nearby.

Back to the task for today, though, reminding myself it was to produce a final line on the map, based on the first of The Spirit's seven signs. My problem now seemed to be with the rivers that radiate, generally eastwards, from the Cairngorm Mountains. Looking at a map of Scotland and only at the river systems, was an entirely new experience - a new dimension. So, I looked at the headwaters of the River Tay and its tributaries and could see that they interfaced with the line already sketched, mainly to the west of Rannoch Moor. Moving purposefully north, it was clear that the River Spey came into this same picture, and that its headwaters also linked with that earlier line. One last question just to be sure: was there any gap between these two, because the answer to that would show whether all the other Cairngorm rivers were in, or out of this geographic picture. Very detailed scrutiny of the map followed, and the verdict was `out`. They were the North Sea bound, nonetheless.

This bit of geographic detective work finally led me to the conclusion that if all the rivers on the eastern side flowed into the North Sea, no matter where their source, then the line I'd sketched must be it, because of the continuity clue that The Spirit had given. To add convincingly a bit of more formal geographic clout, I did several on-line searches and found that both a Wikipedia and a Collins Atlas Survey of about 1912 showed, or rather implied the same line or divide, which I'd just drawn on the map on the floor. I even found a more obscure, but authoritative Gazetteer reference of 1882, that added geographic weight to my efforts, regarding the singular significance of Duncansby Head. I was looking at Scotland in an entirely new and exciting way; I'd discovered what might even be described as a new-take.

Positioning my map as near to the laptop as possible, a very detailed piece of work followed, in which I plotted the precise line on my digital map, by considering all the rivers, tributaries and burns in all the upper reaches of the associated river systems. By choosing a bold red line to mark the map, the next three hours were spent slowly plotting the centre of 'the lands above the waterheads' from the border with England to Duncansby Head in the far northeast. It was a difficult business, with no time to contemplate all, of the landscapes that the line embraced. There were many moments of frustration when I took a wrong turn or two and had to delete a section and then re-draw, adding convincingly to the ever-lengthening red line.

By teatime and exhausted, the line was complete, so with a great sense of relief, the laptop was ceremoniously shut, and I went into the kitchen to make the dinner. After an afternoon at the University, Liz would be ready for something to eat.

Everything was ready for Liz when she came in at around five, and no sooner was she across the threshold than my piece-de-resistance; a fish pie was being served-up for the occasion. The salad had been prepared earlier, and I'd got a tomato loaf to go along with it all. We sat in the kitchen to eat this and finished off some remaining cheeses with oatcakes. There was also a glass of wine to accompany this basic, but fine meal.

Exchanging the news of the day while we ate, I said I'd arranged to meet Ronald at seven, and asked if she'd like to join us.

"Yes, that would be grand, I`ll look forward to hearing more about your quest, as no doubt that will be the main topic?"

"Eh, yes, and it`ll be good to get your take on it as it unfolds, on paper, that is."

Gathering laptop, maps, and notes together, we headed out for the short walk down to the Sheraton. Ronald was there waiting for us and had managed to get a reasonably sized table with seats for us.

After the usual pleasantries and exchange of live news on this and that, we got down to business. By giving him a brief re-cap on the strange and almost incredible circumstances under which I`d received the Seven Signs, he asked a couple of rather searching questions about the manner, age, and sensibilities of The Spirit, he seemed satisfied that I wasn`t making the whole thing up. It hadn`t been just a figment of my storm-battered brain.

"I`ve not done anything with the necessary information you gave me earlier Andy, as I wanted a fuller picture from you first."

"And although I`ve heard some of it already, Liz chipped in, "I haven`t heard of what Andy`s been up to on the kitchen floor today. So, I`m all ears, as whatever the outcome or conclusions, I`ve no doubt whatever, that it`ll have some impact on me in some way."

Fishing into my document bag, I pulled out three copies of the Seven Signs that I`d printed out earlier. Both looked at their sheet and the clues on it with some puzzlement. Ronald commented that it was, on the face of it, quite a conundrum.

"What I reckon for openers is that the first one is just that, the starter; it's there for a very real and fundamental purpose. So today, I spent a lot of time with a big map of Scotland which amongst other things, has land elevation and the rivers marked on it. Important to note, that rivers always start on the higher ground, as water always flows downhill."

"Had to assume that every word there is deliberate, and has some exact meaning and relevance. While that is probably true of all, of the Seven Signs, I'd concentrated solely on that first one."

Although the lounge was busy, with people and waiters coming and going, none of this seemed to be a distraction as I gave Liz and Ronald a blow by blow or river by river account of my prior research; I had their rapt attention. Each sat in silence taking in all that I had to say. Liz perhaps appreciated it in a more visual way given her artistic bent, while Ronald seemed to be tuning into the logic of it, with that degree in philosophy behind him and his career in journalism.

"I never knew that you'd so much geography in you Andy," Liz quipped light-heartedly."

"Well it's been a steep learning curve, let me tell you."

Ronald was clearly deep in thought and did consult the Seven Signs paper from time to time. Then, when I had rounded it all off and paused for breath, Ronald gave his verdict. "Even if we went to meet some Professor of Physical Geography, he would come to the same conclusion. You, my friend, have cracked the first puzzle, and you are also correct in assuming, that the others will follow on in some way from this. My round, to celebrate, I do believe. Liz, another wee glass of wine, or a malt perhaps?"

"Oh, hell yes, Ronald. I've not got an early start in the morning. Thank you, I think a Highland Park if they've got it, would be lovely, thanks." Liz said enthusiastically.

"Same for you, Andy?"

"Yes, lovely, thanks."

The whisky was ordered and consumed with due reverence; I stood and raised a toast to "The Spirit."

Liz then asked, "so what are you going to do with this, now that you've worked out the first part?"

"I'm rather thinking aloud here, but Ronald has kindly offered to carry out some research and do a bit of his skilled delving. So, I think I'll select possibly half a dozen different and widely spread areas, on this watershed, or the lands above the waterheads, explore them, discover the spirit of place, get some photos and email notes to Ronald to pull together with his investigations. Then we'll see what to do with it."

"Oh, will you, now?" Liz said rather coldly. "So, you're going to be away stravaiging for weeks on end, are you?"

This pointed question took me by surprise, so I realised a bit of caution would be in order. "No, not for weeks on end, but several shorter trips, Liz. That's what I've in mind."

"That's a bit better, she replied. "Having buggered off in a tearing hurry without even telling me beforehand, has justifiably given me reservations."

"Let's talk about it later." I prompted a bit cautiously.

"Yes, that's a very good plan, Andy." She said taking another reassuring sip of the malt.

Ronald intervened by saying, "Listen, I'll do whatever you think is best. I'm keen to be entirely helpful, in a positive way. This venture intrigues me, as I believe that it's onto something quite new and exciting. Just keep me posted."

The conversation then roamed across the other clues, with our speculation varying from the sublime to the fantastical, in friendly hilarity. Ronald rounded things off by impressing us with his Gaelic and told about a hill called Druim nan Cnamh, which he informed us meant `ridge of the spine`, that perhaps we should bear this in mind when looking at the line of the map, that I`d just folded up. We were, as he reminded us, "talking about the spine of Scotland."

Liz was rather quiet as we walked back up the road, and our conversations were decidedly muted even when we got back to her flat. My caution prevailed too as I knew that I must be sensitive and considerate in making any plans. Back to the settee, once more.

By the time, I surfaced in the morning, Liz had gone out to meet Hermione and the girls. A hint, perhaps, that I should get myself back to Peebles. I did, however, take the opportunity to produce a schedule of my planned outings to five well-chosen locations on the watershed; the real start of my quest. Printing off four copies of this, I took one and left the others on top of my tray of assorted things that I kept on the kitchen worktop.

Chapter Five

Those next few days were a whirlwind of activity, partly to put a bit of order back into things, but I also suspect it was an attempt to take my mind off the mental and emotional turmoil I was in. The high which gave such a real buzz was the quest, with its novelty and purpose, while the low, was the difficulty between Liz and myself. Answer: keep busy.

Going through all my outdoor gear, it was cleaned, sorted, counted, and serviced, with the new stuff I'd purchased in such a hurry integrated into my well organised kit store system. With a full and demanding day of mountain biking on the forest trails a few miles along the road next day, I got some of the tension out of my system. Nice to be back on my proper mountain bike.

Ronald thoughtfully came down to Peebles for a day in which we discussed the quest in much greater detail. Using my schedule to set the scene, we mapped out where I'd be and when, and what kind of information he could expect from me during and after each outing. For his part, Ronald outlined how he would go about trying to make sense of Signs two to six, with an assertion that we must come back together to number seven, the eco-spiritual one, to a conclusion. With a good lunch, plenty of chat, and a sound plan under our belts, we acknowledged a day well spent. Ronald was pleased to be reunited with the gear he'd so cautiously lent me in something of a hurry, and I assured him it was all there, cleaned, and ready for his use, before he departed.

On the Wednesday, I set myself the big physical challenge of a circumnavigation of the hills surrounding the Manor Valley. If the distance, combined with the succession of ascent and descent in this huge horseshoe was demanding enough, the unceasing wind and rain tested my resolve.

The following day, Liz's sudden and unannounced appearance really took me by surprise. Although we'd exchanged a few brief, if blandly neutral, and just informative texts, in the interim, I'd no feeling that things were showing any sign of change. But there she was, on my doorstep.

"Right, Andy Borthwick, I've discovered that you can be a stupid eejit, but let's see if there's any way of progress beyond that fact. The weather is more promising now, let's go off up a hill. Tinto will do fine."

As we climbed Tinto together, the silence between us was oppressive; one of us would need to bridge it if we were to make anything of the opportunity we'd created in agreeing to go for this walk.

It was Liz who took the plunge. "There's something almost irreconcilable about where we are at right now Andy, and I don't like it. Not one bit. Dear God, I can see why you want to do this quest of yours, and why shouldn't you. You've probably earned the indulgence. You did act in one mad thoughtless way last week, though, but I'm getting over that a bit, perhaps."

Listening in silence, I was surprised, hopeful, and despairing all in one melee of conflicting feelings.

"Let's see how the Sunday lunch this weekend works out. You're not uninvited, and you are my partner, for the event. I find that I just cannot get you out of my mind or my system."

"I do hope we can restore things between us Liz."

A surge of gratitude raised my spirits, but only temporarily. Then Liz changed tack.

"I've been speaking to Hermione, and she acknowledges that Jamie's pretty hard to live with these days. His attitude and manner have changed somehow, he`s even more uptight than he`s always been, with a growing obsession about the conservation and land-reform mob, as he puts it. So, his problem, whatever it is, is not of your making. But to have this tension between your interests and his obsessions festering in my family is unbearable."

"Don`t know if I`m reassured about Jamie`s apparent position. Not much we can do to change that. Maybe he needs help."

"That's as maybe Andy, but I need your absolute assurance about two things. Firstly, I must insist that you`ll not seek to provoke him in any way on Sunday. Just keep out of his way as much as possible. And secondly, that you`ll be there for me and my exhibition in the summer. I`m going to need your help and support. Can you promise me these two things?"

"Of course, I can Liz, and I do. I`ll do my part. And you can count me in for your exhibition. I`ll be back from my quest safe and sound, and in plenty of time. Ready to wield a hammer and screwdriver."

"Surely Charles and Lorna`s wedding at Mar Lodge will be another time for great family happiness and celebration too. And that's only a week or so away. Am I still invited to that?"

"Yes, as once again, you are my partner, for the occasion."

Climbing Tinto together seemed to have worked a little way for us.

Returning via Peebles to pick up some of my smarter clothes for the lunch, we then went out for dinner together to a bistro we liked in Bruntsfield. This meal was most enjoyable, and our conversation appeared to restore a little of the bond we had shared. Back at Liz`s flat, there was a further turn that took me a little by surprise. Deliberately suppressing any lingering confusion in my mind, I entered fully into the spirit of the opportunity.

"Think I feel a shower coming on, Andy. Make yourself very much at home."

"`Mind if I join you Liz, a bit of steam together would be nice, If that's OK?"

Afterwards, rolling over beside me, we turned to face and hold each other in a long warm embrace.

In the days that followed, our relationship appeared to have returned to at least something of its former understanding. Liz went about her work commitments; I did a few repair jobs about the place.

In a hurried visit to the Royal Scottish Geographical Society in Perth next day. I`d hoped to get a deeper insight to Scotland`s watershed but came away with little information of any real value. What I did get though was a surprise sighting of Jamie coming out of a grotty pub, in the company of a dishevelled looking man. A bit older than Jamie, he had the appearance of a gamekeeper, but nothing in the grubby clothing matched, and he most certainly needed a shave. Jamie, in contrast, was his usual smart professional land-agent looking self, with everything neat and colour coordinated. Standing in utter amazement at seeing him there, and in these circumstances, I darted back into the doorway and watched in puzzled surprise at the incongruity of it all.

Deciding to say nothing to Liz about this sighting of Jamie in such an out of character location and company, I reckoned it best to continue to work at more relationship building, or recovery perhaps. This endeavour was helped that evening when she suggested we take a wander up Arthur`s Seat, and on the way, asked about those of the Seven Signs we'd not discussed. So, we settled down side by side, almost on the rim of Salisbury Crags.

"Geographic discipline is one thing, but what about the more-subtle landscape characteristics? I can see that if we are focussing on the lands above the waterheads, the terrain must all be on the higher ground, and must, therefore, include a lot of mountains and tops. What do you make of the one about deep peat, Andy?"

"Well, there's a lot of that on the watershed Liz. How often have we been climbing or trekking the high ground when we've encountered bog, lots of it in a big squelch?"

"It's more than just that though, I've been giving this a lot of thought, trying to imagine your likeable, if obscure, Spirit character and the key to his, what can we call it, message, perhaps? With all that we now know about the importance of deep peat bog for both carbon capture and wildlife, mainly birds, I think we're convincingly reminded that it's utterly central to landscape and therefore human survival. And the fact that The Spirit singled it out, suggests to me that of all the geographic features he could have picked, the Watershed is unique; it has a disproportionate amount of the stuff surviving on it, and we should do more to appreciate it. There, that's my thesis on this one Andy."

"How right you are Liz, and I value your take on it. We are I do believe, singing out of the same song sheet."

"Yes, but whatever you, we, and I include Ronald in this, do about your discoveries, we must make sure that bog or peat get all the attention that they should. While I know that rivers have a very special place in folklore, there's almost bound to be something about how our ancestors viewed bog land and the spirits that they knew dwelt in it. And that would be both bad as well as good ones; I've no doubt. Unfinished business for me, at any rate."

"This seems to lead almost seamlessly onto the next, the fifth of the Signs. Keywords in it are surely diverse, least cultivated, and empty. It seems to me that we need stronger physical evidence of this, and that's where my exploratory ventures come into it Liz. Although I suspect that I know something about what I'll discover if we are going to confound the sceptic, and vested interests which we know exist and are just mustering for action, it's the hard evidence that's called for here. Ronald said something about looking at the way in which all land in Scotland is already fully classified for its agricultural potential, so I want to add the aesthetic description and moving images."

"Yes, that appeals to me Andy. I feel a photographic account coming on too."

"Hey, that would be good my love; we'd be on the case together."

"Just so Andy Pandy, but remember it's me that wields the camera, and let's just say, has the eye to use it, to good effect."

"Of course, you do Liz, but I like the idea of this bigger exercise being one that we both play our respective parts together. In it together, dare I say."

"Steady now, but that same song sheet will play a great part."

"Before we leave it and move on to the next, I just want to stress that I'll be looking for diversity, for sheer variety of habitats on this Scotland-long ribbon in our landscapes."

"The mostly uninhabited nature of it appeals to me Andy, and the signs of abandonment, where we human beings reluctantly gave up on it as a place to live on, or even near. There are ghosts to be encountered. Good ones, I mean."

Moving a bit closer together on the clifftop we sipped the wine I`d stuffed in my pocket as we were leaving her flat, and chatted. Liz continued with an enlightening and well-informed discourse on folklore and symbolism in landscape shape and texture, which took me by surprise.

This lovely lady knows what she is talking about, came over loud and clear, and for me, moved her place in the whole endeavour up a notch or three. She seemed to be bringing our forebears right into the core of the landscapes we were talking about, and by implication, gave The Spirit and his wisdom a place that enriched the human state.

"Well, you`ve pretty much answered the last of the Signs for me, Liz. If we get attuned to all the other Signs, their meaning, their core place in our environmental understanding, and how if we will but let them, they`ll be an authoritative guide to how and why we must love the land, the human dimension will be profoundly enhanced. There, simple as that, I`ve made my, our, pronouncement on the Seven Signs, and there`s no turning back now, whatever the weather."

Chapter Six

Sunday lunch with Hermione, Jamie, and their two girls was certainly something to look forward to as we drove towards Aberlady. Hermione always puts lots of effort into creating an elegant spread for this family institution, and all the more-so when visitors were to be there too. We were to be joined by her parents Archie and Marissa and could anticipate some pleasant conversation I reckoned, as we approached the house. There was no reason to believe that this occasion would be otherwise.

An array of cars was already parked outside what I called this assertively modern house. Jamie came out to meet us as we drew alongside an ostentatious people carrier. He embraced Liz in an excessive way, which rather matched his personality in so many other ways. And when it came to me, a formal and fulsome handshake was accompanied with "Come away in, lovely to see you both, we`ll have time for a wee drink before lunch, I`m sure."

Entering the house, we found that it was comfortably warm, with the sounds of voices coming from the sitting room, and further down the hall, in the kitchen. A light aroma of cooking food drifted through and helped to set the scene for the meal. We were enthusiastically ushered into the sitting room where Archie was deep in conversation with Monique about her school work. Charlotte was sitting over by one of the windows and quietly engrossed in a book. Both girls were in their Sunday best, as they`d been to church. Archie stood up as we came in, walked towards, and greeted us.

"Well, hello Elizabeth and Andy, its lovely to see you. I hope you are both well, though I hear you've taken a bit of a step into the unknown". He said looking directly at me.

Liz thankfully took the initiative and replied: "Hello Dad, great to see you," As she embraced him. "Where`s Mum?"

"She`s in the kitchen helping Hermione to get the meal organised"

"Hi there, Charlotte and Monique". I said enthusiastically.

"Can I get you drinks?" Jamie asked very sociably.

"I`ll have a sherry please" Liz requested," Dry if you`ve got it."

"And I`m driving so I`ll just have a sparkling water, please Jamie."

"OK," he replied. "Monique was just telling me about some of her school work. She`s got some exams coming up."

So, Liz went over to her, to continue this conversation, and I went over to Charlotte and asked her what she was reading.

"It`s an Anne of Green Gables book." She replied quietly. "I don`t have to read it for school or anything like that, I`m just enjoying the story. My friend Christine lent it to me. She said she`d liked it."

"So, what does Anne get up to in this story?" I asked, eagerly.

"Oh, she`s involved in all sorts of things. At the moment, the bit I`m reading just now, her pony has gone lame, and a Gymkhana is coming up the next weekend, so she`s anxious and wants to get some help to have it treated properly. Anne is so eager with her pony and wins lots of prizes. She`s very popular. Everyone loves her, except a girl called Sonya, she`s quite horrid and jealous really."

The conversation had only just started when Jamie butted in and said: "I'm sure Andy doesn't need to hear about the squabbles between Anne and Sonya, dear."

I was about to say that I was keen to hear more about Charlotte's book, when Archie appeared with my drink.

"Here you are Andy, one sparkling water. Very commendable of you."

"Hope I can hear more of the story later Charlotte" I whispered to her, as I was ushered away to join Jamie and Archie over by the fireplace.

"So, I hear you've packed in your job, and even your stability." Jamie said, with the hint of sarcasm in his voice. "What on earth possessed you to do that?"

"Oh, there's been a whole lot of changes in the way the authority goes about filling just about every job, and even at the level I was in, they made it necessary for me to apply competitively for my job, the one I'd been doing fine for a good while. And a waster called Mike, who's known to swing the lead oversaw the whole selection process, so I decided I'd had enough of it all. There and then."

"But a job's a job, man, probably with an excellent pension package thrown in, because it's the local authority or is it civil service." Jamie snapped. "You'd have been much better to take whatever they offered, and see how you could move forward with that. And it'd have been much more secure for Liz, should she ever want to settle down and stop work, had you thought of that?" He demanded.

Archie cut in, "Well I'm sure Andy knows the politics of local government much better than we do. He'd that to contend with. I've seen the effects of it through one of my colleague's legal practice, and it's a bit of a nightmare, with one review after another. Andy`s a resourceful chap; I`m sure he`ll find something to move on with."

"What are you going to do?" Demanded Jamie, not willing to let it go, or be deflected.

"Tell you what, I`m sure we`ll go for a wee walk on the beach after lunch, I`ll give you a bit of an outline then." I replied in good humoured vein.

"Excellent plan." Said Archie. "I think lunch must be about ready to be served, as I hear lots of clunking of dishes."

I was beginning to like Archie; a thoughtful pragmatist, which was a lot more than could be said of Jamie.

"I`ll check," said Jamie, drifting through the dining area that adjoined the sitting room, to the kitchen beyond. He re-emerged a couple of minutes later and announced that lunch would be served in a few minutes if we`d like to take our places at the table.

Liz had been deep in conversation with Monique about her school work, and the words `art project` somehow came out of the flow of it, so I could imagine that they`d have lots to discuss. Charlotte had returned briefly to the safety of her book, and Archie gave the logs on the fire a poke with his shoe, before replacing the fire-guard. He stood back somewhat stiffly. We all picked up our drinks and went through to the dining area.

Jamie rather formally issued instructions as to where each of us should sit; it was all carefully thought-out. As we were making our way to our allotted seats, my eye was drawn to a fine big painting occupying pride of place above the sideboard. I`d been informed on more than one occasion that it been saved from the family`s Spurryhillock House, before that once fine building was abandoned to the elements. The picture was a Highland landscape, with all the necessary components of crag-girt mountains, mist, a small river in the valley, some sheep grazing beneath a rowan tree, and a shepherd, of course. I liked it, but Liz had said that she didn`t; not to her taste.

With Archie sitting to my right, and Jamie at the head of the table, Liz to my left, and Marissa opposite, I surveyed the scope for conversation, as that was regarded as an important part of these occasions. Archie was from an old landed family in The Mearns, and while he still owned the Spurryhillock Estate, the farms were all let out, and the old Georgian mansion, a forlorn ruin. The family retained the home farm, as a larger than usual holiday home. He was a senior partner in a long-established Edinburgh law firm, and Marissa worked part-time as a PA in what had recently been re-branded as Creative Scotland. They lived in a very comfortable house in The Grange area of the capital; wearing their considerable affluence with reasonable modesty, however.

When Hermione served the soup, Jamie stood up to say grace. This formality and Christian overtone was not part of my everyday experience. But it appeared on this occasion, to be observed with due reverence by all.

"Eat up, everyone" Marissa invited. "And do pass the bread around Jamie".

After a brief silence, as everyone made a start on their soup, Jamie asked the girls if they`d enjoyed the church service in the morning. As fifteen and thirteen-year olds, I did wonder at the word `enjoy`.

Charlotte however responded quickly, commenting that; "the Minister had told a rather corny story about a tramp and his dog, and the need for us to be kind to all animals as God`s creatures.

I suppose he's right, but since I don't know any tramps, it seemed a bit peculiar to me. And there was a lady sitting a few rows in front, who kept blowing her nose and making a noise with some sweets from a bag. I'm never allowed sweets in church. Did you see that?" She enquired of Monique, who was sitting beside her.

Before Monique could say anything, Jamie cut in; "That's a rather flippant way of telling us about the church service Charlotte, I'd have expected more from you."

Thankfully the awkwardness that Jamie's response had created, was quickly broken by Liz, "Yes, I remember some of these children's stories in church being a bit corny too, Charlotte. There was one that I recall . . .

Marissa quickly cut in with "More bread anyone?"

This gesture diffused the tense atmosphere which seemed to be hovering over the occasion, and I could see that while poor Charlotte was pleased the attention had been diverted away from her, she was embarrassed by it all.

Archie then said; "well I'm very much looking forward to our summer break at Home Farm. August, isn't it? I've had a couple of new showers installed, and believe that they look a bit like the kind of thing you'd expect in a good hotel. Now you girls will approve of that, I'm sure. And Hermione, I think you'll like the new Aga that is being put in to replace the old one."

"Yes, that does sound lovely Dad, said Hermione enthusiastically. "It will make living in the place so much more comfortable, won't it girls?"

Liz then commented that she'd try and come up there for a few days, but it would be around the time of her Festival Fringe exhibition so that things might be a bit tight. She'd see what she could do, though.

As Hermione cleared the soup dishes and brought in the main course, Marissa asked "Oh tell me about your exhibition dear, have we provided you with any funding for it? Where is, it going to take place? I'd love to come and see it."

"It's a Fringe event like hundreds of others that are on at the same time Mummy, so there's no chance of us getting any grants for ours. It's going to be at a pop-up venue in the Three Sisters in the Cowgate, and I'm sharing it with my friend Christine. It'll be a mixture of my photographs and short poems to go with each. Also, hope to put in special lighting and sound to it. There's still a lot to do to put it all together. But Andy here's promised to help with this. Christine is not bad in digital design, so she'll handle the publicity. Probably a lot of social media stuff."

As the roast beef, Yorkshire pudding and all the trimmings were served up, Marissa continued. "That's very nice dear, but I'm a bit worried about the Cowgate as a location to hold it. Isn't it a bit grubby down there?"

"I don't think you need to worry about that Mummy, during the Fringe the whole place is a buzz of activity, with shows and exhibitions happening up every close. And each night, they hose the whole street down with big powerful pressure washers, a bit like what you see in the American movies."

"Oh, I see," said Marissa, sounding very unconvinced.

"Is the beef to everyone's liking." Hermione then asked. "I do hope so. I promise I'll come to your exhibition Elizabeth, will get one or two of my pals in the Art Club to accompany me."

The formal use of Liz`s full name certainly reflected their parent`s traditional approach.

Funny how different two siblings and their choice of partners can be, I thought. Although cautious about myself, so that I couldn`t be entirely objective on this, it was clear that Hermione appeared to want the solid one hundred percent respectability, a man who`d earn money for her and their children and be home of an evening to complete the scene. Whereas Liz, who`d had much the same upbringing and opportunities, wanted something very different, much less restrictive as she had often told me, and found fulfilment in being creative and in the rejection of materialism. I knew she wanted the world to be a better place and was willing to put herself out to make it happen.

"That would be nice Hermione. If you let me know when you are likely to come, I`ll look out for you, and once you've had a look around, we can go for a coffee." Liz replied while being a bit doubtful if it would ever happen. Her sister made no secret that she didn`t think much of either her work or her lifestyle.

Once pudding had been served, Archie volunteered a story in an effort, to lighten the atmosphere. "I`d a meeting with a rather wealthy client during the week, who wanted to make some changes to his will. Not that he anticipated dying anytime soon, you understand. He`s well-known and a scallywag of an Edinburgh character."

What promised to be an indiscretion on Archie`s part drew everyone`s attention. But mischievously he dashed all our hopes on that, by saying; "now I could tell you who he is, but I really shouldn`t, so I won`t. Sorry to build your hopes up." He said, with a bit of a twinkle in his eye. "Anyway, he wanted to ensure that his wastrel of a son...."

"Mummy what's a wastrel," asked Monique out of plain curiosity.

"Oh he's someone who spends money he can't afford or hasn't even got, now don't interrupt your grandfather dear," said Jamie.

So, Archie continued; "yes, his son has turned into a real rogue, and keeps needing to be bailed out by his father, my client. We'll call him Mr. B, for Bernard, but of course, that's not his real name, though it could be, you'll never know, now will you?"

An air of impatience circulated, as this was all shaping up to be an Archie tale, but he continued. "So Mr. B knows that his son will have a right to a goodly part of the estate on his father's death. But he wants to get as much of it tied-up in some way, and the rest of it squirreled away so that there will be much less for the son of B to get his hands on in the end. Mr. B knows his son would just squander it. So, he and I talked a bit about that likelihood and came up with some ideas and plans, that I assured him would be just within the law. Mr. B looked quite pleased, not to say relieved. But then he put a bit of a spanner in the works by adding, that he had a mistress, and our hero wanted her to be provided for, very adequately, as he put it."

"Mummy, what's a Mistress," asked Monique, again with real curiosity in her voice.

Archie was about to reply, and got as far as; "a mistress is." When Marissa jumped into the story with a; "really Archie, you know you shouldn't be using words like that in front of the girls, and not at the lunch table either."

Charlotte looked even more interested at this apparent naughtiness by her grandfather, and added, "But I was only asking". And then looked a bit offended.

Archie picked it up again by saying; "Ask your mother later, what it means."

At which point Hermione looked flustered, but did say to Charlotte; "yes dear we'll have a chat later if you like."

Archie then went on with his somewhat interrupted yarn. "I said that what he should do is make a monthly or annual payment to her, or buy her property as an investment for her, but that this payment would be a risky one, for obvious reasons. He'd must just accept it as a risk. And that it would be for her to decide on how she deals with it tax-wise. I also added that it would be better if Mr. B were to live for at least another seven years to avoid any more Tax-man scrutiny than would be wise. Business concluded, we went off for what turned into quite a long lunch together in his Club. My parting shot to him as we rolled along Heriot Row was; 'Your money should be safe now Mr. B/As we've performed a few tricks don't you see. There'll be hard-times for your son, and your lady will have fun. The tax-man will just have to agree."

The company erupted into laughter, though Marissa did round it off, by saying "Really Archie, you are a rascal, and that's not really a fit story for the Sunday lunch company." But she ended her apparent criticism with a chuckle.

When things had settled down a bit after Archie's tale, Hermione turned her attention to me and asked in a rather cold manner; "what on earth I planned to do with the rest of my life, now that I'd resigned from a safe and secure employer. And it had such a good pension lined up? It seemed to be most unwise and irresponsible. I'd hoped you would settle a bit more and devote more time to Elizabeth, and your future together."

This had rather put me on the spot, but I knew I'd come up with something that would at least appear to buy a bit of time. So, I said "Och, I'll spend a few weeks rambling the hills, and that will perhaps clear my thinking about what I want to do next. The way The Outfit is going, under this Tory Government, I don't think any job is safe." I could see out of the corner of my eye that Jamie bristled at this comment of mine, but ploughed on. "Yes, a few weeks with my boots on, a pack on my back, and map in my pocket will get the work situation and its machinations right out of the system. The weather is looking promising too, so I'm sure I'll emerge from the wilds with a real clear focus on things. Of course, I've promised Liz to help her with her exhibition. That'll keep me busy until the end of the Fringe. No need to worry about me Hermione, I'm excited about the next wee chapter."

Marissa then came in with; "yes dear, excitement is all very well but it doesn't build a future, and you've got to think of these things, especially as you have an, eh, a partner," she said rather awkwardly.

"Well, let's just call it something of a bit of a gap-year, only a bit later in life than is the norm. Didn't Hermione have a gap-year with VSO or something?"

Jamie, who'd been rather aloof from all these discussions, stood up and announced that coffee would be served a bit later, once those who would like to have had a walk along the beach. "Lovely afternoon for a stretch of the legs, and the dogs could do with it too."

"That was a lovely lunch Hermione, thank you so much," Marissa said. "Yes, delicious, wouldn't you all agree? I'll help you to clear up."

There was a lot of nodding of heads, and sounds of agreement, as one by one we stood up, stretched, and made our way through to the hall to collect sundry coats, boots, hats, and walking poles.

The dogs that had been sitting quietly in the kitchen responded to this sudden flurry of activity and started rushing about excitedly. Jamie got their leads, and so we headed out into the afternoon sun, determined to work off some of that lunch.

The girls ran on ahead, chattering and laughing between them. Both were quite tall for their age, or at least they were both growing up rapidly. They showed some of the usual differences between siblings, with Charlotte rather more like her mother in temperament, and Monique showing similarities to Jamie. Both had somehow changed very quickly into more casual clothes for this beach outing.

For better or worse, we quickly fell into two pairs, with Archie and Liz walking along together, giving them a bit of father and daughter company and chat. There seemed to be a natural flow of conversation between them, and a keen interest by each, in the other`s lives and interests.

Jamie and I found ourselves together, a little behind the others. Immediately sensing that I was in for a grilling from him, because I knew full well, he was never happy that Liz and I were not married, and didn`t miss an opportunity to say so, or drop rather barbed hints. The fact that we didn`t want to get married, and had agreed between ourselves, that it wouldn`t suit our respective life-interests, seemed to wash over Jamie`s head. I`d almost got used to this tedious obsession about this and just concluded that must be a misplaced older brother thing. It certainly didn`t suit his perceptions of where his sister should be in life though. The informality of our relationship somehow offended his apparently Christian mindset too. He was after all an Elder in the local Kirk and certainly wanted it to be known amongst us that this was one of the key measures of his respectability and place in this community. The recent onset, or emergence, of his tense manner, didn`t help.

Getting in there first, though, I asked him how things were going at work. He was a chartered surveyor and land manager with McDuff & Parker, a long-established company, that seemed to be a favourite of the older landed families, many of them titled. He was happy to re-assure me; "that their aristocratic acres would be safe in his hands."

"These are strange times," he said. "The value of land is ever increasing, and of course there are great opportunities to make money from renewables. But these bloody conservationists are forever making it difficult for us. And as for the so-called land reform people, it's a bit of a nightmare. What's wrong with the way things are? But we'll fight back, as we have always done in the past."

He certainly seemed to see himself as very much part of all this, and personally too, with his use of the word `we` to define his place in it.

"I was up north this week at a lovely estate we've been working with for many years, in the Loch Rannoch area. The General, who owns it, fifth generation in his family I believe, is a lovely old man. Still, works as a solicitor in Edinburgh some of the time, but he really should retire. I was looking at some plans to make the estate more fit for his retirement and develop the sense of privacy. With a bit of judicious planting and construction of some big wide drains, we should be able to at least frustrate access to his policies, by the nosey public. We've got a good man on the ground there; a kind of general factotum, ex-military. He's occasionally a bit unpredictable, but we get on well, so he'd do anything for me, oh, I mean for the General, of course. Yes, a grand project that one."

Dear God, I thought to myself, the auld guard is certainly alive and kicking. But I said nothing. Just added, "Yes Loch Rannoch is a lovely area, and becoming increasingly popular in all sorts of ways."

Jamie frowned at this, and I could see he was wondering if it was a wind-up.

His turn to mount the inquisition. I knew I was in for it, but my loyalty for Liz meant that I was most unlikely to deliberately seek any falling-out with Jamie, even if I did disagree with much of what he represented.

"What`s all this about packing in your job, man," he started. "May not have been much of a job, but it was indeed secure, and you could have made more plans with Elizabeth. Now that's all up in the air, I`d say, and that is not fair to her. An ill-thought-out decision, I`d say."

Don`t mince your words mate, I thought.

"No worries about Liz and me, we are fine, we`ve talked things through, she`s very content with the current position. I`ve promised I`ll be around for the exhibition, her first big public break. That's her immediate need, and I`ll be there for her."

"That's not what I`m on about; it`s you and her in the longer term that I`m much more concerned about. Elizabeth is thirty-seven years old, as you well know, and she should have a settled future."

I decided to shift the focus away from Liz and me, as I simply didn`t want to get stuck in yet another discussion of this sort with Jamie.

"We`ve agreed that I`m heading for the Highlands for a few weeks, well, a bit more than the Highlands. I`m on a quest to discover something new and big about the landscapes of Scotland." I decided to press on with this account of my plans, as I didn't want any dafter interventions from him. "I have some clues to follow, that I got from a mysterious ancient character that I met in Rhidorroch. These clues and there are seven of them, are about defining something quite original, focussing on continuous wildness, running the entire length of Scotland. Worked out what the first clue was the other day, and a journalist friend is helping with the others. But it's all to do with the character of a strip of land, a line on the map which my informant called the lands above the waterheads. This continuous strip of land is where the centre part of the most of the major river systems have their source; it's a watershed, the watershed of Scotland in fact. The whole venture is a challenge, an exciting quest to unravel the mystery, to explore parts of it, and identify how these clues do show that it is of real environmental significance. Rather surprising really, that it hasn't all been done before. If we asked people in The States about their watershed or big divide, they'd have plenty to talk to us about. But there it is, an almost unknown environmental gem right in our midst."

"No matter what you may think of these things, Jamie, Scotland needs real, far-reaching emblems, icons of the finer qualities of our landscapes. In fact, I think we can derive an eco-spiritual experience from this. We, will if we choose, benefit much from it. The new Wild Land Areas that the Scottish Government has defined, are part of this, and the work of so many great conservation organisations play an active role too, for a lot of their members and the public. If, as I'm on the quest to discover, there is something that can pull all this together in some way, with a bit of joined-up thinking, we're on the verge of a monumental leap in how we can enjoy our wilder landscape. I know it's all sounding a bit woolly for now, but ..."

Jamie cut-in; "I'll say its woolly, it's also on a different planet. And if you get all the information you want, and your journalist pal writes about it in the papers, or worse, will this create a reason for yet more people to go tramping all over the place, carving paths across the great estates and frightening the deer? If that's your goal, it sounds horrendous to me. It's the very last thing we want or need. It smacks of the more extreme end of the so-called land reform bunch, most of whom live in the cities, for heaven's sake. We in the countryside know what's best for our landscape and indeed for conservation too."

His reaction had been predictable in some ways, but the severity of it took me by surprise.

"Well, Jamie we'll just have to see things differently, but I know this is in-tune with a far wider spectrum of the community than you seem to be. I'm quite undeterred by your reaction to my plan for the next few weeks. Going to enjoy stravaiging all over the place to achieve it, be sure of that. It'll serve its purpose too, in putting bureaucracy right behind me."

For once, Jamie seemed at a bit of a loss what to say. We had by this time walked some way along the beach, and turned around into a cooler breeze. The others were all well ahead of us. Liz and Archie still deep in conversation, the two dogs running this way and that, and the girls not far behind, with whoops of laughter coming from them.

Jamie launched in one final time, as we came to the point on the beach where the path to the houses started.

"Disagree we most certainly will. I'm not especially interested in your airy-fairy notions, but I am deeply concerned about the implications of folk being encouraged or sanctioned even, to wander all over the place in pursuit of your idea of wildness." His tone was nothing, if not hostile, and I had an uneasy feeling.

"Oh, there's nothing airy-fairy about what motivates me, it's all based on sound environmental principles that are well researched, and will at the very least limit the damage we do to our planet. I'm just appalled that the interests you represent are in denial, and either can't or won't see what is glaringly obvious, that the current state of land management, and yes ownership, in Scotland is an ecological downward spiral."

Arriving back at the house we came in to warm chatter, coffee, and cake; cake, we were told, to celebrate that both girls would be playing at the school's end of year concert in the Usher Hall; Charlotte on her violin, and Monique on piano. A full-size concert grand sat lid-open in the bay window.

"This cake is delicious girls" proclaimed Marissa. "Well done in being selected, and we all wish you well."

"We do indeed," said Archie; "and look forward to being in the audience to hear your performances."

Both girls looked a bit embarrassed with this attention being lavished upon them.

After the cake and all the pleasantries, the party was over, so we bid our farewells, with due thanks to Hermione and went our ways.

On the way, back to Edinburgh, I commented that; "Jamie seems quite irrationally opposed to my quest."

Liz was once again expressing open hostility to the plans, summing it up by saying "Anything that risks driving a wedge between that family, my family, and me, is simply not on, Andy. Sort your priorities."

With cold hostility in Liz`s attitude towards me once more, and after yet another night on the settee, I got the bus home to Peebles.

Chapter Seven

Launching into; "when are we leaving on Friday to go to the wedding?" Liz's phone call took me by surprise, once more.

"If you still want my company at the event, Liz, I'd suggest we head north from Edinburgh just after lunchtime."

"OK, well you'd better get yourself up here on Thursday, so things aren't rushed on the day. Your kilt is waiting here for you, and so am I."

Although I was back once more into a state of confusion and didn't want to force things with any ultimatum, this roller-coaster was wearing. I just wanted to be certain of things, to be able to get on with my very peaceful eco-quest, and have a consistent relationship with Liz; one that I could be sure of.

The journey to Mar Lodge was uneventful, the accommodation there was quite luxurious in a very corporate Scottish Highlands kind of way, and the whole event got off to a grand start, with the formality, ceremony, finely attired gathering of guests, and a fitting sense of occasion for Charles and Lorna's wedding. Liz and I kept any difficulty that there had been between us well hidden, I told her that she looked gorgeous, and we got on very well, under the circumstances. She certainly appeared to be enjoying herself at her cousin's wedding, and I found myself feeling pleased for her.

With the formality of the wedding ceremony over, there had been a break to give staff the time to transform the ballroom into a more ceilidh-ready state. During the break, guests had made their arrangements to have a drink, coffee, or nap, and the more energetic had gone for a walk in the grounds. For most, this also gave the opportunity to change into their ceilidh attire, so much more tartan appeared, as folk drifted over in the warm evening air from the main Lodge to the Ballroom. In twos and threes, they gravitated towards this extraordinary structure. On the outside, it looked like a big red barn covered in a lattice; it presented a rather forbidding image. Two pipers flanked the doorway, to proclaim where it is in this otherwise rather blank edifice, and to announce that something of significance is about to happen. The chatter being exchanged in the little groups of guests was eclipsed by the strains of Scotland the Brave, and Bonnie Galloway.

Inside the Ballroom, the scene had indeed changed. Staff had been busy; the tables and earlier decorations had all been removed, and the full expanse of the top-lit but otherwise windowless hall became clear. The walls and ceiling were boldly adorned with hundreds of sets of stag's antlers in a grotesque display of largely masculine destruction, masquerading as sport. As Liz and I entered the hall, we were both a bit dumbstruck, as the starkness of it seemed so overwhelming. In contrast, Liz looked gregariously feminine, her active vitality and personality glowing. She had chosen to have her hair loose for the evening, was wearing a new mid-length deep blue dress, with a belt that accentuated her slim waist. With dancing shoes and no tights, her figure looked captivating. For my part, I was still wearing my Robertson tartan kilt but had substituted the earlier tweed kilt jacket, with a green ghillie shirt and Jacobite waistcoat. Brogues on my feet were ready for some jigging.

The stirring strains of the pipes from outside the door faded as we came in, and were quickly replaced by the sounds of the band warming to their act. I quickly took to the four-piece combination of funky fiddle, flute, guitar, and drums. What I took to be the caller was also on-stage giving advice about the finer points of tuning, amplification, and the positioning of microphones. The banter between the members was light-hearted and served to set the scene for some lively music.

The hall quickly filled, with more colourfully dressed tartan clad guests, and with the addition of those arriving just for the ceilidh. The babble of conversation rose to a mass of lively voices, drinks were nervously retrieved from the crush at the bar, and peals of laughter punctuated the scene.

I came back from the bar, handed Liz her a glass of white wine, and took a welcome drink out of my pint of beer. Then, we were joined by Hermione and Jamie, who had also got their drinks in hand, so we found a table together at the end of the hall furthest from the band, in the hope that some conversation would be possible when, or if, we were not dancing. Hermione was dressed in a similar style to Liz, but her tartan dress was not pulled in at the waist, and she was wearing light green tights with her sensible shoes. A silver brooch that looked like it had a family crest on it, and her hair up, as it had been earlier. Jamie was still in his Prince Charlie jacket and waistcoat above his kilt. His sporran looked very much like it had been made from an unfortunate beaver fur and head. His tie matched the tartan of his kilt.

"Well, this is some place." Said Liz, to get the conversations going.

"Sure is," Jamie chipped in. "The Fife`s owned it all for many years, sold the Balmoral part of it to Queen Victoria, and built this place so that they could still be near the Royal presence. This Ballroom is an exuberant expression of how they viewed themselves, and what you must do when you come to the Highlands. I like it. It`s just a pity that the whole place, including the great mountainous estate, is now owned by the National Trust for Scotland. They are destroying its character."

I felt I had to offer a different view of things, so said "Och, I don't know. If it wasn't` owned by the Trust, there`s no guarantee we`d be celebrating cousin Charlie`s wedding here today. Otherwise, it would probably still be someone`s private playground, with us, the public kept well at bay. And the conservation work on the estate is turning it back into a much better habitat for a range of wildlife." I said confidently.

"Now boys," said Liz; "let's leave the politics of it all for another time and place. We are here to enjoy Lorna and Charlie`s wedding, aren't we?"

"She looked gorgeous," said Hermione. "In fact, they both looked great. The celebrant was so well prepared, and quite humorous too. The happy couple was obviously enjoying it, and I could hear their vows loud and clear. Oh, I do love a good wedding."

The first dance, a Gay Gordons was called, so Liz and I took our places for this favourite starter for a ceilidh. Easy going, couples only, not too intimidating; it gets the event up and running. Not much chance to chat during the dance, so we contented ourselves with just getting into the swing of it.

Hermione had to coax Jamie onto the floor. She was a fine dancer, light on her feet, knew the steps, and clearly enjoyed the set movement to music. He, on the other hand, was a bit awkward and had been in a sullen mood, since I had offered a very different perspective on this estate and its place in Scotland today. Liz and I danced the next few dances together, as did the other two. We enjoyed ourselves, and the atmosphere in the hall was excellent. The caller was doing a fine job from the start, and the band was lively; I took to their funky style and imagined that it probably enabled more people to feel that they could take part, even if they were a bit unsure of what to do.

At first, I thought I imagined it, but Jamie seemed to be taking every opportunity to bump into me, and on one occasion he swung a kick to my calf, that connected. He must have been aware of what he was doing, it wasn't just accidental, but he never acknowledged or apologised. This action riled me.

Hermione and I danced the strip the willow together, and I found that I was confidently guided by her superior knowledge of both the routine and the steps to go with it; this made the whole dance a thoroughly pleasant experience. Liz and Jamie both sat it out and seemed to chat politely, if not enthusiastically.

During the break, I went out, to admire the stars in the sky, as I put it. No disappointment there, as the clear dark moonless sky was ablaze with silver spots, and with no light pollution, it was a truly breath-taking spectacle. Liz had joined me briefly, and we both stood arm in arm gazing. It had got a bit cooler, so she went back inside, and Jamie immediately appeared. He came over to me in a manner that I found threatening and launched into a tirade about those bloody conservationists wrecking everything, and making the running of big estates so very difficult, and more. After pausing for breath, he demanded to know if I was involved in any of them, but before I could answer, he continued; "that he was utterly opposed to my next venture, and why couldn't I just leave things alone, leave it to the real country people?"

I suggested that if we were going to have this conversation, it should be carried on more discreetly around the side of the ballroom building. So reluctantly, Jamie came with me as I moved into the shadows, and out of the way of passing guests. They wouldn't have been impressed with two grown men in kilts arguing loudly. Decided I wasn't going to let him get away with this verbal assault and would make it clear I'd every intention of pursuing the start of my venture in less than a week.

"Don't know what your objection is, Jamie, and what's more, don't care. It's none of your business. I've every intention firstly of enjoying being out on hill and moor for the next few weeks, and I hope to feel that I'm connecting with the countryside too. I'd urge you to keep out of my plans and leave me to do what I want to do. And if I make some interesting discoveries, I'll do everything possible, along with Ronald, to share it all very professionally and publicly. Do I make myself clear?"

"Where the fuck, are you intending to go on all these wild wanderings? Who's land will you be invading and polluting?" He spluttered.

"Again, not that it's any of your bloody business, I'll be in the Moffat Hills, the Campsie's, Rannoch Moor, in the Rough Bounds, on a flow called Knockfin Heights, and that's just for starters. As to who's land, it may be, that is damned well irrelevant."

He took an angry swing at me, but I was ready for it and grabbed his arm, turning him round, and pinning him face-first onto the side of the building. "You, insufferable creep," I yelled in his ear. "There's plenty more of this, where it's come from; damned if I'll be dictated to by some jerk that's in the pocket of the old lairds. They are a spent force here in Scotland today, and with any luck, such controls and influence that they do cling onto will be hammered out of them, and soon." Tightening my hold on him, as he gasped, and tried in vain to swing a kick or two at me, I put my knee firmly in the small of his back. "Now have you got that?" I gasped, as I was running out of wind.

Somehow, he managed to wriggle free, but not without ripping his shirt and waistcoat on a nail sticking out of the lattice. As he got free, he swore again and swung a punch, which hit me fair and square in the stomach. This blow winded me, and he had gained the offensive, as I buckled in a heap on the ground. He kicked out with one of his brogues, and it landed on my thigh with some force. Somehow, I mustered the quick reaction necessary to grab his foot as he pulled away, and I wrenched it round with all my strength. He too fell to the ground in agony, as I wondered if I`d broken any of his bones, with him lying there groaning for some time.

But I was rapidly on my feet and planted my brogue on his chest, without using too much force. His groans mingled with all kinds of profanities that I didn`t think he was capable of, and gasping for air. I too was breathing pretty heavily, but in looking down on him threateningly, said; "I hope that this is the end of it, Jamie you fucking moron. But if you want an action replay, we can have a dual anytime, somewhere more discreet than your lovely wife`s cousin`s wedding, though. You are on dangerous ground. Oh, and just be absolutely clear Jamie Ferguson, although this isn`t the focus of my quest, I want you to know that we need a radical change to the old socially inhibiting order, and to the sleekit land ownership arrangements that often cloaks itself in secrecy." This last point was pressed home with a prod from my heel.

"We'd better get cleaned up somehow, and get back into the hall." So, I removed my foot from his chest, and without halting, walked straight towards what looked like staff toilets near the outside corner of the building. I'd the place to myself, fortunately, so could survey the damage. On the outside, it looked superficial, even if my leg ached. Washing my face, hands, and every exposed part, I straightened my clothing and walked back towards the entrance. Still furious, but I decided the best thing to do was to come clean with the ladies. Jamie had attacked me in an entirely unprovoked manner, and he had lost.

Liz came out of the door, just as I walked up to it, and asked crossly; "where have you been, and where`s Jamie?"

"There`s been an incident of Jamie`s doing, we are both OK, but can you get Hermione, and I`ll explain."

Liz turned, and quickly came back out of the hall with Hermione, and I drew them to the side to offer some explanation. "You`d probably noticed that Jamie was niggling me earlier on, well when he came out just as you were going back into the hall at the break Liz, he started ranting and slavering about my walking venture. So, I cautiously moved us out of the way, to try and calm things down, and to get out of the limelight near the door. At this point he physically attacked me, punched me hard in the stomach and we had a fight. I was understandably furious, and he came off worst."

"But, where is he?" demanded Hermione. "I must see he`s all right, where did you leave him?"

"I left him round the side of the hall, just badly winded I suspect. He`ll probably have retreated to your room to tidy himself up. Would you like me to come and help you?" I said doubtfully.

"No, you will not, you've done enough damage for now" At which point she burst into tears, and Liz scowled severely at me. They went off together to find Jamie.

Going back around the side of the hall to check if there was anything left there, an empty silver hip flask was lying on the grass. It wasn't mine, as I`d come without, so guessed it must be Jamie`s. Using what little light there was, I could check out the surrounding area, and found my skian dubh, at which point I thought, it's a good thing it fell out and into the darkness.

The ceilidh was obviously in a good swing, as whoops and the odd screams were in competition with the sound of the band, but I headed back to our room, to clean up a bit more. As I was walking along the corridor, Liz came out of Hermione and Jamie's room and came towards me. I signalled that we shouldn't talk out here, and we went into our room, closing the door firmly.

Chapter Eight

Subdued by the events of the evening, Liz seemed reluctant to accept my fervent assurances that I'd not provoked the attack in any way; this doubt from her hurt, almost as much as the wounds Jamie had inflicted. Trying in vain, it seemed, to comfort and reassure her; I found myself having to call up all my resources.

"How could you allow yourself to get into a fight, at my own cousin Charles`s wedding? It was supposed to be an entirely happy event, and it was going well, until Jamie, and you set about each other. Between you, you spoiled it, not just for me, but for poor Hermione too. You broke the spell," she railed.

"Dear Jesus, I did not set out to provoke or antagonise him in any way, Liz. I knew from this morning that he had it in for me, when he told me aggressively, that I`d better watch my back. I just let that one pass in a light-hearted way, but believe me, I did watch my back. Did it as much for you Liz, as for myself, I didn`t want this great day for you, ruined."

"If you`re so adamant about this Andy, how on earth did that fight start?"

"Och, I`ve already told you, and that's the way it was. He was aggressive and threatening from the outset; even kept bumping into me and kicked me when we were all dancing, just before he attacked me. Tried to reason with him but politely made it clear that my plans were my business, not his. It was at this point that he took a swing at me, and punched me. Well, I wasn`t going to accept a doing from him, so I had, to retaliate. But believe me, love, it was reluctantly, and in such a way as I hoped would not wind him up anymore."

"I'd like to believe you Andy, but whatever happened between you turned into a melee, more fitting for a pub at closing time, not my cousin's wedding. God, I just hope not too many people saw this scrap. That would be the last straw."

"Once I realised he was serious and intent on being violent, I steered us around the corner of the hall, and out of sight. Drink probably fuelled some of it, 'could see that he'd been tucking into the stuff. Here, here's his empty hip flask that I found on the grass afterwards. There's no reasoning with a drunk, is there?"

"Reasoning or not, drunk or sober, it degenerated into a mad punch-up. Now he's hurt, Hermione's mad, and we can only hope that the girls slept through all its aftermath. How much had you had to drink? Did that contribute to it in any way?"

"You know fine well, that I was and am cold sober. I'd taken it easy on the drink, for you Liz. I did not want anything to spoil this day, for you."

"Well spoiled it is, and you were in the middle of the spoiling of it."

"Well, now that we are into the recriminations Liz, I'm going to defend myself and my actions. In addition to the fact that Jamie was a bit pissed, I do believe that he has lost the plot. It's a psychiatrist he needs to see. I'm deeply sorry for Hermione, she didn't deserve any of this, but it was her husband, fair and square, who instigated the whole thing. For fuck's sake, haven't been in a fight since I was at school, and you know yourself that I'm normally a peace-loving sort of bloke. You've said so yourself. I just don't do aggression very well. And the fact that you are giving Jamie any credibility in this; the fact that you doubt my word hurts like hell. Sure, this places a huge strain on your loyalties and family ties, but it was, not of my making. I'm afraid your sister has married, well I doubt if she knows right now, what she`s married to, but it's not pretty."

As Liz lay on the bed, still wearing that lovely dress, she`d wrapped a blanket around her, whether for protection or comfort I knew not.

"I`m deeply sorry that things worked out as they did Liz, it was absolutely not my intention. Jamie must have come here looking for his misguided opportunity, and drink provided just that for him. I love you, as I always have, and I want us to survive this. But I cannot be expected to capitulate to a mad-man like Jamie. He needs help, urgently."

"Oh God, how do we dig ourselves out of this hole. How are you going to get us out of it Andy?"

"Haven't a clue right now Liz, wish I had. I've come across this utterly destructive behaviour as part of my work with stoned seventeen-year-olds, but never expected it in what I regard as my family. Could offer to give Jamie the benefit of a bit of counselling, but I doubt if that offer would be well received."

"Too true it wouldn't. I just hope the new day has a brighter perspective on things when it comes. But there`s a long night ahead."

Still pumped-up about the whole business, I did my best to comfort Liz, and sometime about first bird-song, must have fallen asleep.

That Jamie and Hermione had left Mar Lodge sometime before any breakfast was possible, came as both a shock and raised not a little alarm to Liz and her parents. Some explanations were offered but received with doubt. Not much hope of me being able to help matters at this stage, I set off for a walk, and to give me time to think. Thankfully none of the other guests seemed to have the same plan.

Walking alone to Linn of Dee in the morning, the quiet beauty of the route just washed over me; I saw none of it.

The whole situation was deeply depressing, and I found that it was impossible to resolve any part that I may have had in it.

It was clear that Jamie had crossed a line, and created a scenario that would be hard, if not impossible to come to terms with. His utterly irrational and then violent behaviour seemed to me to push a little personal disagreement into a dangerous place. How can you reason with that? I asked myself, as I plodded along with a heavy heart? He seemed to be oblivious to the effects that this would undoubtedly have to his immediate family; especially his wife and children. That he seemed equally oblivious and indifferent to the impact, it would have on Liz, and our relationship troubled me greatly. Short of him recognising that he needed it, and receiving professional help, I could see no way out of the mess he'd created. What worried me more, perhaps, was where it would lead? If this was what he could do at a family wedding, then what of the wider world that we inhabit?

With these and so many other dire thoughts, I started to reflect on the wisdom of pursuing my mission. Would I be better just to call it all off, or had things got to a kind of Lady Macbeth point of dilemma? Doubting that I could go back, and thinking of the promise that I had made to The Spirit, I felt trapped. But my entrapment was not of my making, I reasoned. Oh, didn't mind losing face, and just admitting some change in direction, but, why should I?

How could I help Liz; she was the one person above all else that mattered most to me? She hadn't done anything to stoke the problem. Having doubts about my part in it last night was perhaps fair enough, but with any luck, we could work our way through that. She was deeply hurt, and I desperately wanted to do something to help her. Few people would have any sympathy for Jamie, his actions, and what he represented politically, other than a few far outdated landed families, perhaps. Any rational person would see that he had become unhinged in some way, that he was utterly abdicating his family responsibilities, and inflicting immense damage all round.

As I reached the bridge over the deep dark pools at Linn of Dee my mind was still filled with an incoherent jumble of conflicting emotions; my thoughts were probably almost as distracted as Jamie`s. Looking gloomily at the watery depths, I could see no beauty in it. I stood there staring into the abyss for I knew not how long, and tears rolled down onto the stone parapet, making puddles of sorrow. This despair somehow prompted yet darker thoughts, with a fleeting memory of death and loss among the hills of home in Galloway. But I suppressed it, as there was quite enough grief to contend with here, right now.

The gloom was given a start, with the impatient tooting coming from a large people-carrier, who's driver clearly thought I was obstructing the bridge. Moving sufficiently to let it past, I looked further down the river to where the pools spread into turbulence, catching the tormented light, and moving on. This distraction from my deep dilemma was just enough to get me moving once more.

The sombre return journey was taken at the same ponderous pace, but I did find myself to be thinking perhaps a little more clearly.

Just three thoughts seemed to prevail from the jumble of despair that had almost overwhelmed me on the way up to the bridge. Jamie came first in my resolve to sort out what my priorities were, or do something about things that must be sorted. This plan is simple, at one level, I could do nothing about the fact that he had lost his reason, and caused a dreadful problem thereby. I could not change him, or his actions, and I was not going to be held in any way responsible for this.

My quest was a gentle and harmless one, and no matter what it provoked in Jamie's sadly warped mind, I would press on as planned. A much greater good would come from it; my faith in it was being restored.

It would be much more difficult to restore Liz's faith in me, though; her loyalties were being tested, perhaps to breaking. But I determined more and more strongly with each footfall on the way back to the Lodge, that I would do everything possible to recapture and sustain our relationship. We had been together for long enough for me to know that she'd have no admiration or respect for my moral fibre if I just gave in to this weird external pressure.

As I was nearing the rear entrance drive to the Lodge, a car came along behind me and stopped. Turning around, I could see it was Liz; she must have driven the longer way around to find me. Pulling into the side of the road, she got out and came over to me, and my level of anxiety soared. I could quickly see however that there was no need to worry unduly, as she embraced me. Clearly, something had happened to change things.

"I'm so sorry to have wandered off like that this morning Liz. I needed my space, and to try and sort things out in my head a bit."

"Shh, no need for apologies Andy. Things have taken a turn which confirms that much of what you had said to me back in our room last night is probably correct. Jamie is now in a psychiatric unit or hospital in Perth."

As we drove the short distance back to the Lodge, Liz explained that Jamie and Hermione had set off in the middle of the night, but not before she'd entrusted the girls to another cousin.

"They'd got about as far as Perth, and Hermione had thankfully been driving. Jamie had been raving, so in desperation, she went to the Police there, where by luck a doctor who'd been in attendance for some other reason, saw the situation, and just took charge of it. Jamie didn't seem to be aware of what was happening, and again by good fortune, a bed was available in the local unit, so he was admitted. Whether he's been formally sectioned or not I don't know, but anyway, Archie has gone down to be with Hermione, and Marissa is waiting for us. The girls may be there, so we'll just need to play this by ear."

In such contrast to our journey north just two days earlier, our return home was going to be marked by a mixture of foreboding, relief, and cautious hope.

Marissa had got a lift with the other cousin, her husband, and the girls, so their needs were taken care of, for now. She had shown a slightly frosty acceptance that I had been seriously wronged in the doings of the previous evening. "Let's leave it like that, for the present." she had said rather curtly. Liz and I had found a quiet corner of the Lodge to have coffee and scone before setting off; continuing our discussion as she drove us down the road.

"I'm so sorry I doubted your word last night Andy, you deserved much better than that of me."

"No apology needed Liz. It was clear how it may have looked, and you must have been torn apart by the conflict of it. Let me tell you about what I resolved, as I was walking back from my thoughts and feelings of despair at Linn of Dee. There's probably still a puddle of sorrow on the parapet of the bridge there. But, as I looked down into the darkness of the water there, it was a dark place. Anyway, I was jolted out of it by some impatient bugger in a big black car."

"So, I decided three main things, which almost complement each other, starting with my utter love and commitment to you."

By the time, I finished, although mutual exhaustion was creeping in, to my immense relief she said "Our love will weather this one, Andy, I'm confident of that. As for Jamie, you are right, you're not responsible for the way he is, and you can't change him, `nor should you even try. Carry on with your quest, it is at the very least, harmless. And it's your special venture. From where we are now, I'd have been unimpressed if you'd let Jamie deflect you."

Chapter Nine

With deadlines looming, and her exhibition only a matter of weeks away, Liz knew that there was some urgency in selecting the photographs that she'd want to use. She was acutely aware too, of the need to make any final technical adjustments with tone, light, and colour on them, and only then being ready to take the plunge to send the final images away for printing. This method would have to be done on a Fine Art standard of card to obtain the quality of photo prints that she wanted. A company in Newcastle would meet her exacting needs, she told me.

To start this process of selection, she printed out her top fifty images onto A3 card, took them home and laid them out around the edge of the living room, hall, and kitchen floors, propping them against items of furniture, door frames and whatever would hold them up ready for scrutiny and selection. With a whole-day ahead of her, Liz set about narrowing the fifty prints down to the top thirty. `No panic`, she thought to try and reassure herself, but this is my first big display event; it is the shop window on my work. Then there`s the three lines of poetry to be added to each image, and last, of all, there`s the critics. Oh, dear God, am I ready for all that public scrutiny? Nothing for it, but to make the selection and move on from there. Better make it good.

Armed with coffee and the occasional biscuit, Liz went around each one, recalling where it had been captured, the conditions at the time, and what she`d been trying to achieve. There were images of a scattering of leaves in a turmoil of light, shade, and colour; a hills scene with sinuous overlaid shapes given varied emphasis by sunlight and shadow; the trunk, limbs and branches feeling their way skywards only to be lost in the over-reaching green canopy; texture and shades of grey with lichen on rocks; sunset over a western isle; sunrise touching the rim of a jagged horizon; footprints in the snow; Nature had provided her with an opportunity, in every case.

There a was joy for her in the results captured and fixed on each page. While in some cases Liz frowned with frustration at the perfection that had alluded her. More coffee and another biscuit helped her go around each room, as she stood close to scrutinise, or back to admire. She was completely absorbed in the photographic potential of the natural world she had captured; or had she indeed created, as it lay around her, and drew her in. Only fleetingly did she glance into the more troubling events of recent weeks, but immediately returned to this artistic form that for her, for now, eclipsed all else.

Slowly, the images moved from room to room, as the very best migrated with her careful consideration to the sitting room. The ones she would reluctantly have to let go were finally relegated to the kitchen, and the ones that were hardest of all to adjudge, even after some hours of her attention, lay in transition; in a kind of no man's land, in the hall.

After a very brisk walk around The Meadows in the rain, followed by a soak in the bath and finally some food, she returned to complete the task in hand, with a new vigour and critical eye. The phone rang; she ignored it. Something popped through the letter box; she let it be. People passed by on the street outside, and the sounds of children playing in the back greens; none touched her concentration.

As at last, the daylight began to fade, and exhaustion crept in, Liz found that the hall had been slowly cleared of the less suitable prints. The kitchen door was shut, and she could relax in the sitting room, with a glass of wine while listening to a CD with the very fitting sounds of Land of the Mountain and the Flood, by the aptly named Hamish MacCunn.

After the trauma of Jamie's performance at the wedding, I urgently needed to have a real burst of fresh air on the first of my quest ventures: in the Moffat Hills.

Warmed by the thought that any journey to the higher places is fuelled by a sense of anticipation, excitement even, this one had the added edge of being the start of something big. Heading south took me through many familiar glens, but this venture had an extra new purpose. On the way, I felt a rising passion for the course that The Spirit had set me upon; it was as if my life had found a new route to be followed. Where it would lead at the end of the day, I hadn't a clue. But the immediate task was clear; to explore the higher ground, the lands above the waterheads; in this case, between the sources of Tweed, Yarrow, Moffat and Annan waters, near a high-level moor with the unlikely name of Rotten Bottom. The mission was clear, the descriptions and photos would follow, I was fit and well equipped, and my motivation was leading me on to a small but significant part of this, Scotland's enduring and continuous wildness.

A night and a day were spent on a high, allowing myself to feel closer to the landscape than ever before, perhaps. I took delight in the detail of a single flower, or in the texture of the wider landscape, and pleasure in the warp and weft all that I could discover, that made it what it was. I must have been in a self-induced trance, for I imagined the very rocks singing an anthem on evolution, age, the seasons of the sun and moon, and the sheer timeless magnificence of Nature.

As if to cast a blessing on my mission, the weather was clear and warm for the time of year, making the journey into the terrain and all its attire, a joy. Puffy clouds from the south-west drifted slowly across an otherwise clear blue sky. The shadows that they cast produced an ever-changing light and the passage of time was measured only by the almost imperceptible movement of the sun in relation to features upon the horizon. Flowing lines of hill upon hill paraded around the perimeter, with gaps revealing yet more distant views into more spreading valleys in a mosaic of greens and browns. The deeper steeper foreground lay in sharper focus, with what appeared to be an intense higher resolution, while the further and yet more distant hills were accentuated by sensuous shapes; layer upon natural layer. The ever-evolving panorama in the round, was captivating, and the higher ground as I explored from hill to hill, changed gradually with every step, or so it seemed.

Camera and notebook were rarely at peace, as I sought to capture as much as possible of both place and purpose.

Later in the day, I sent Ronald as much of this as I could within the limits of the battery life of my phone. What he would make of my perhaps incoherent ramblings and random photos, only time would tell. Time now though, for some food and rest in this high place.

Lying there in my contentment of a day well spent, with a full belly, and a deep familiar satisfaction of camping high and wild, my mind ranged over those evening signs and their profound connectedness. Yes, they pulled together some of the finest environmental threads within the lands above the waterheads in a very long web spun entirely by nature, but they brought together both our growing understanding of ecological imperative and the much older lore about landscape and people. How had all that emerged, I pondered? Not from knowledge as we would recognise it. Perhaps not even from a purely human view of things either. In my trance like state. I seemed content, reconciled, to an almost spiritual dimension to what I was exploring and experiencing. The tantalising gift of time with the immense complexity of nature must surely challenge our assumed and arrogant superiority. What the mysterious Spirit had so humbly ventured, and entrusted me with, could if understood and cherished touch the human soul; it could become a potent symbol.

Carried along on by these and so many other similar thoughts and feelings, I must have finally drifted off.

Sometime in the small hours, however, this calm was shattered.

Slowly emerging from a haze of confusion and uncertainty I became aware of pain, severe discomfort, and then the cold, I opened my eyes to darkness. Then closed them again, perhaps to give myself time to take stock of my situation, or perhaps to blank it out. Nothing made much sense, but I seemed to be alive, in pain and feeling very cold; it must be night. Then wondering what had happened to get me into this state, I remembered the fire around me while I`d been in my tent.

Gradually straightening myself up, but still lying on the heather, I hoped to get a better idea of how things were for me. My face felt very hot, in contrast to the cold air around it, and the skin on my hands had been scorched, but they seemed useable. Didn`t think I`d any broken bones, but did have a very strange taste in my mouth. My breathing was returning to something like normal. Fumbling in the pocket of my fleece, which had a crisp layer on it, suggesting that it too had been scorched, I retrieved my head torch; miraculously it still worked.

Sitting-up awkwardly I surveyed the scene. There was still smouldering heather or peat beside where my tent had been, and my loose items that had been in it hadn`t fared well. My rucksack, however, was looking intact, if blackened. My water bottle was lying beside me with the top off, so I picked it up and was about to take a drink from what was left, but it had a strange smell coming from it. It seemed that it might not be pure water at all, so I put the top back on and reached for the other smaller flask in a side pocket of my rucksack. This water tasted much better, and a couple of big mouthfuls helped to restore my senses.

Shining my torch around the area where the tent had been, I could just make out a more scorched circle of heather; there had been a ring of fire created around my tent. I was beginning to remember things now. The faint sounds of someone moving around the outside of the tent in the evening had awoken me from an after-dinner nap. No, it hadn't been fully dark then. Must have shouted something, and moved quickly to unzip the doorway, and vaguely remembered rolling through the porch area, as the whole tent erupted in flames behind me. Had I seen someone running off across the moor? I wasn't sure. But I did recall grabbing my water bottle for a drink and looked in utter amazement and shock as my tent disappeared, a ring of burning vegetation around it smouldered. I must have passed out.

Realising that I'd been attacked, by someone with very malicious intent, and which was the last thing I'd have expected high up in these hills, or any hills for that matter, I was in shock. But just sitting here wasn't going to help my predicament. The assailant might even come back, to ensure that he'd done what he'd set out to do, and that must have been to kill me. The question of why, would need to wait, but I could think of no good reason.

Standing up and realising I could walk, I decided to gather up what gear there was which might be of some use and crammed it in my rucksack. Still by torchlight, I then tidied up the other burnt remains and put a couple of rocks on top. There was an odd smell around, in addition to the burnt plastics of tent, sleeping bag and all the rest. On getting down closer to the ground, I did a bit of sniffing to see if I could identify it. Following it around the scorched circle outside the site of the tent, I realised it was continuous, and that it was none other than paraffin.

Some biscuits had survived in another side pocket of my rucksack, so I ate them, put the flask of polluted water in another pocket, and set off to find the fence that I knew enclosed the whole of the Carrifran Valley. This aid would provide me with a clear handrail to guide me down to the road, and to safety.

Still, in a state of utter shock, I carefully made my way along the side of the fence, reckoning that it would be more reassuring than the path I'd come up in the first place. The going was very rough in places, and I stumbled over many a rock or clump of heather. Some areas of very wet bog were hard to traverse, and before long, both boots and feet were thoroughly soaked. As I stumbled along the beam of torchlight swung wildly from ground to sky in a hideous sweeping performance. Coming to a major corner post where the fence turned sharply left, there was some comfort in reaching this landmark in the dark. That comfort was soon abandoned, though, as the route started to fall away steeply. A good juncture at which to take a break, take stock, see if I could find any more food in my bag, and use a little more of that precious water.

The realisation that someone had tried to kill me was beginning to register. Sitting there in the dark, and still feeling the cold, the stark reality of what had happened but a few hours earlier, hit me hard. Dear God, I thought, I'm used to dealing with young criminals, many of them violent, and murderers amongst them, but that was in one world; tonight's experience was utterly different; it was very personal. I'd never been on the receiving end. Oh yes, the odd punch or kick, but I knew how to deal with that effectively, it came with the territory. The worst had been when someone bit me, hard, and as a result I needed to go and have an Aids HIV test. But an attempt, and a very real, deliberate one at that, to cremate me in my tent in an isolated place; someone really had it in for me. I was in a dark place, both literally and metaphorically, the outcome of which might be a journey in a wooden box; couldn't even begin to comprehend this.

The night air was getting to me, so I had to abandon the questioning and get myself to a safe place, as soon as possible. Early light was beginning to emerge over the hilltops on the other side of the valley.

The descent took much longer than the ascent just forty or so hours earlier. My hands were already very tender from the effects of the fire and rapidly became raw with grabbing the fence to prevent a fall. Knees, elbows, and shins all got a bit of a hammering, with regular stumbling over obstacles hidden in the dark. As I got nearer to the road, however, the way was getting a bit clearer, so I did transfer to that well-trodden path. It was just as well, as the battery in my head torch had expired. My eyes adjusted to the new situation relatively quickly. Leaving the hill behind, and crossing to the farm steading, the only sound was a dog barking. Announcing my arrival, or survival had not been in the plan, but it seemed to be a whole lot better than the alternative. Thankfully I`d left the keys in the wheel arch, so could quickly fumble for them, and get on my way. Hadn`t a clue what time it might be, but guessed it might be around five o`clock.

Once in the car, which I`d to remind myself Liz had kindly lent me, and driving up the road, I needed to start thinking straight, because some bastard had tried, nearly succeeded, to murder me.

The combination of fire and poisoned water was no mere accident. Must report it to the Police, and consider whether I needed any medical attention. Right, Police first, but where? Nearest would be Moffat, but that was taking me in the wrong direction. Selkirk would be next best and would be getting me nearer to home. The road was thankfully empty, with nobody else out at this hour; so, no witnesses to my slow and erratic driving.

Arriving in Selkirk, perhaps an hour later, it took a while to locate the Police Station, as I had to find someone to ask for directions. Eventually, I found a newsagent that was just opening for the day. The lady was busy carting bundles of newspapers into the shop when I asked her where I might find the Police Station. She chuckled at first while saying "Well I`ll give you directions, but it's more of a Police house with an office attached to it. You might be lucky." Then looking me up and down, she said "Holy God, what happened to you, son? You look as if you`ve been in a fire? Are you OK?

"Yes, and yes. I mean I have been in a fire, and I think I`m OK. Thank you for asking. I need to report the incident to the Police first.

"Right, I`ll not keep you back from that. The local Policeman is Jim Armstrong, and his house, I mean office, is along to the end of this road, then first left. He`s a cousin of mine, so I`ll phone him right now to tell him you`re coming his way. What's your name?

Armed with that information she disappeared back into the shop, and to the phone I presumed. While I then made my way slowly and cautiously to PC Jim Armstrong`s office.

A rather bleary eyed semi-dressed Policeman came to the door after a few minutes. "Come in, and I`ll get some notes from you about what has happened. Through this way please;" as he ushered me into the office. "Strictly speaking I shouldn't` do this as I`m not due to be on duty for another hour and a half, but I always, well almost always do what my cousin Shona says. Let's get you a cup of tea first." He disappeared through to what I took to be his kitchen, and came back shortly with a tray, laden with teapot, milk jug, mugs, and biscuits.

"Many thanks, Jim," I said, as he handed me a mug of tea, and pushed the plate of biscuits in my direction.

"How did you know my name`s Jim? No, don`t tell me, Shona told you."

"Yes, she did indeed."

"You look a bit singed and scorched, and your clothes look like they've had a very close encounter with fire, but are you OK, do you think? Because if you do need medical help, that should really come first."

"No, I think it looks worse than it is, on the surface at least. I guess it's what might have been that's a whole lot more worrying."

At this, he got his notebook out and started taking the usual essential personal details, ending with next of kin. That always sounds grim and ominous, I thought.

"Tell me what happened, and how you come to be in this state. Just start at the beginning." He seemed to be selecting which parts of the tale to record. In between taking mouthfuls of this sweeter than usual tea, and eating more biscuits than would be normal, I recounted in what I hoped was a sensible order of events. Jim nodded, scribbled, and gave the odd `OK` or `Oh really`. But it was when I got to the arson that his attention focussed. Pursuing some more detailed questioning about this, there followed by more frantic note-taking.

Pouring me another mug of tea, I suggested a bit less sugar this time, as I reckoned the first shot had been a good enough fix.

"Have you any idea at all, who may have done this to you, any idea at all, will do? The offences that this person has committed, and I mean plural, are pretty serious, and it would be a good idea if he, or she, was caught and put out of circulation for a while."

"No matter how much I've thought about it Jim, and I've had a good three hours to do so, I cannot for the life of me think of anyone who might even remotely be responsible. Camping up there could have offended no one. I`ve no real enemies that I know of, in fact, everyone comments on what a likeable sort of bloke I am. It's a mystery, a blank."

Reckoned it was best to leave Jamie out of this. As far as I knew, he was still in hospital having flipped, and in any case, he just wouldn't have had it in him to trog to the top of a steep hill in the middle of the night with a can of paraffin and a box of matches. Anyway, how on earth would he have known where I was last night? No, Jamie was surely not part of this crazy event. One little detail did niggle, though, and that was that apparently one of my schedule lists had apparently gone missing from Liz`s kitchen. No need to go into that right now, though.

"And you say you saw absolutely nobody at all during the day or evening."

"The only person I`d spoken to was a farmer that calls himself Bodesbeck, who invited me to park my car in his farmyard rather than it cluttering-up the farm road-end. Oh, shit, he`ll be thinking I`m still up the hill, but the car has gone."

"Don't worry; I'll give him a call, and just let him know you've headed home a bit earlier than planned."

"Thanks for that. I don't want my stravaiging the hills to cause any anxiety to anyone, especially someone as helpful as this Bodesbeck guy. Mind you the events of the last few hours have sure as hell moved the whole thing up a notch or two in the anxiety stakes."

"They sure have Andy. I'll do my report, talk to my seniors, and we'll see what our inquiries will reveal. Guess we'll need to send someone up there to have a look at the arson site. Can you show me on this map where it was? I have this rather ominous feeling that searches and inquiries are going to be a bit fruitless. I know that area reasonably well, and there are many different directions from which to get access to it. You chose a good spot if you don't mind me saying?" I'm finished with you here, and Shona has asked me to send you back to hers for some breakfast. She'll be off duty from the shop soon. I'll phone and let her know you are on your way."

"Oh, and what was it you said your occupation is?" Jim said, glancing at his notebook.

"Perhaps I didn't. I'm between jobs right now, but was until very recently worked with young offenders."

"Hm, you'll be seeing the offending part of it from another angle altogether today. A less sympathetic one perhaps," he replied, with a smirk.

Well, there was to be no arguing with this, but I was not one to complain. This local hospitality was hard to beat.

Shona was waiting for me, as I walked into the shop, and greeted me enthusiastically "Right Andy, I've asked Martin to get some breakfast ready for you, we live just around the corner."

"This is really very kind of you Shona; you didn`t need to go to all this trouble."

"Hey, no trouble at all, it's you that's in trouble, or been in trouble, and need a bit of Selkirk sympathy and friendliness."

She was a fit looking woman in her mid-forties, healthy complexion, glint in her eye, and only slightly smaller than myself.

"I've got some more respectable, less fire tainted clothes in the car."

"Later, you must eat first. Then you`ll be ready to get yourself spruced up. Where is it that you live?"

As we entered her house, just off the main street, a Martin man stepped forward to greet me, but I pointed to the poor state of my hand when he went to shake it.

"Jings, you've been in the wars, boy. Food first; there`s some fresh porridge, and I`ll do you a bit of bacon and egg. Tea or coffee?"

"Wow, this is kind indeed. A wee bit porridge, yes, please. Small fry up would be grand, and tea, will all help set me up."

Seated comfortably at their kitchen table, food started to appear courtesy of Martin. Shona sat opposite and asked just enough to get the gist of the story.

"Well I hope they get the swine that did this," came Martin`s response. "I've never heard of anything like it in this area before. We`ve lived here all our lives, and know the community well, especially the people up the valleys. Where you were, may be just over the County boundary, but it's all one community. We don't take kindly to visitors being treated badly, and violence like this is an outrage. My cousin is a herd up Yarrow, so I'll be asking him if he saw or encountered anything. "

"Now you are fed and watered; you mentioned something about getting spruced up for the journey home. Could Martin get your things from the car?"

"There is no need, but I'll accept your kind offer just the same. There's a scorched rucksack, holdall, and pair of trainers in the boot."

And with that, Martin was out of the door clutching my car keys.

"Right let's have a quick look at the obvious damage. Off with that fleece, or what's left of it, and your shirt. Don't worry there was a time when I was a nurse. Now I'm more interested in saving the planet."

What could I do but obey?

After a good inspection, she pronounced; "that I was incredibly lucky, as the singes and a little scorching were reasonably superficial. Time will do the business, but I'd urge you to go to the health centre as soon as you get home. Eyebrows and lashes will regrow soon enough. But I don't know about your wits. They'll have had a shock. Do you live alone, or have a partner?"

"Yes, and yes, I live alone in Peebles some of the time, but my partner Liz is in Edinburgh. So, I'll head for home, and then for Edinburgh."

"Fine, if she's any kind of a partner, she'll know how to restore your spirits."

With that Martin returned and announced that he'd put my stuff in the bathroom, for me to do as best I can with whatever is in the bags.

Reappearing ten minutes later, I felt a bit more respectable. Although a shower would have been good, I was a bit cautious, as I wasn't sure how even warm water would feel on my hands, cheeks, and forehead. I'd wait till I got home.

Over another cup of tea, and one of Shona's scones, I told them a bit more about my quest, as she seemed pretty interested. Her announcement that she was saving the planet had chimed for me.

We exchanged the usual means of communication, with a commitment on both sides to keep in touch.

"If you need any of the environmental troops mobilised just ask. I mean for the environmental stuff. We'll leave most of the criminal part of it to Jim and his Polis friends."

Thanking them for their great hospitality, I said that perhaps my wits were a just a little bit restored already.

Chapter Ten

By the time, I'd waited to see the nurse on Monday, it no longer seemed necessary, for apart from still not having any eyebrows, much of the scorching had cooled down a lot. With a bit of self-prescribed moisturizing cream to the affected areas, some continued discomfort, and the need to have cool showers, all was slowly recovering.

The Police had been in contact the day after my return home, looking for a few more details about the route I'd taken to where my torched tent had been. Some of this was hard to be specific about, as I'd been exploring; something which doesn't necessarily have a route plan attached to it. They got what I could remember of, though.

A while later, a phone call from them informed me that the few charred remains I'd abandoned under the stones, had been brought down as evidence, should a case ever transpire, and they reported that an empty paraffin can had been recovered from Gameshope Bothy. Fingerprints unlikely, but Forensics were working on it. A very faded label on it suggested a link with a long-abandoned stone quarry somewhere north of Aberfeldy. Not much to go on then. Whoever had done this looked like he or she had got clean away. More questions about any theories, I might have.

"None"!

Liz had come down to see me on Sunday, almost as soon as I told her of my high-level misfortunes, and damage to my wits and gear. She'd Hermione and the girls with her, but they went off on a shopping or ice cream hunt, leaving Liz and me together for a while.

"Great to see you, and thank you making the journey to here to check me out."

"Hey, I`m not just checking you out, Andy. This attack is way into a league of its own. You are in danger."

"It kinda looks that way, and it's worrying, very unsettling, but I won`t be deterred. Anyways the Polis are on the case. They want to get to the bottom of this as soon as poss. It's, well, very reassuring to have the them on your case, with all the skills and expertise they can muster."

"I always knew that you are made of tough stuff with a determined streak in you, and this confirms it more than ever. But are you sure it's wise to be going on with it? Continuing with your quest, I mean?"

"Don`t know much about the wisdom of it Liz, but fuck sake, I`d be letting myself down, if nothing else, if I gave into whatever, or should I say, whoever has it in for me. Believe me; I`m going to be extra ultra-vigilant in the future. But no changing the plans.

Anyways, I see you have Hermione and Co with you. What`s the craik, how are they, and I take it Jamie`s still in hospital? There, that`s enough questions to be going on with."

"They`re fine under the circumstances. They`ve moved to our folk's house in the Grange, plenty of room for them there. Jamie hadn`t been sectioned, unfortunately, so he discharged himself on Tuesday, and just went back to work on Thursday as if nothing had happened. As soon as Hermione heard from the hospital that he`d walked out, she packed some bags for the girls and herself, summoned my help, and left a note for Jamie saying something to the effect that `You`re on your own, but you`ll have the dogs for company`. That`s it. He`s still in a mess, even if he doesn't see it that way, and it is entirely of his own doing."

"Hm, this is all a pretty rapid turn of events, but I can see it removes some of the stress for you all, for now anyway, gives a bit of time for a more permanent solution, and protects the girls from what could be, is, a nasty business. I imagine you`ll feel you can be of more direct help if needed, this way, Liz?"

"Yes, but I think Hermione and the girls will settle and perhaps come to terms with what has happened. Mummy seems to love having then around, and Daddy will have great fun cooking up more of his brand of mischief. What are your plans, though?"

"I`m heading for the far north in a few days, and only for just a few days, I promise, so was going to ask if I could come up to Edinburgh, to yours tomorrow? I also want to meet up with Ronald."

"Course you can, I`d love that. Is there anything you`d like me to take in the boot of the car, so you don`t have to cart it up in the bus?"

"Are you forgetting, I`ve got your car to bring back to Edinburgh? let's find the gang, and go for tea and buns together somewhere."

I knew that the local Police were working thoroughly on solving the crime.

Meantime, Edinburgh beckoned.

Lingering nervousness about our relationship meant that despite her very best efforts to reassure me, I was not yet fully reconciled. It was certainly a complex situation. No longer just about my hasty unilateral escape to the hills, I just couldn`t get over the ways in which Jamie had put the proverbial keech on things, or the extent to which this had put a strain on quite understandable family loyalties. It was clear to me that I`d just need to keep working at it, to restore that which had been lost along the way. Despite all this, though, Liz and I enjoyed the time we had together and made the very most of it.

In the dark unsleeping hours of the night, I found it impossible to ignore so many things; the mortal danger, relationships, a basic sense of responsibility, and this rather abstract quest of mine, Liz, plans – if I had any; none clear and not much resolution.

But the grey dawn seemed to bring somehow a fresher purpose, enlivened by the sounds of the first blackbird echoing around the tenement walls and back-greens. It seemed to sing to me, that evil and defeat can conspire if they will, but the best in the natural world and the human spirit must and will win through. The refrain grew stronger as another bird joined in with assertive songful desire for the new day; the effect on me was clear. I would work on those things that mattered most and do everything to sustain the best in the relationships I cherished. I would honour my commitment to The Spirit, and in solving the mystery of the Seven Signs create a new well-spring for human renewal from the most natural of sources.

Liz must have woken me from a brief sleep with a gentle kiss, that seemed like a benediction on the positive outcome of a troubled night. As I responded and smiled, I just quietly said to myself: `I do hope so my love, I do`.

Meeting up with Ronald, early doors in our usual place, we secured a decent sized table, to spread things out a bit if need be. Once the pleasantries were sorted, we got down to business. For his part, he had begun to tease apart the meanings in some of the signs.

"I want to get my head around the processes and timescales involved in the geological and glacial formation of Scotland, as I guess that will give me a steer on how and when the watershed as we have it today, was formed. It's a kind of multi-dimensional jigsaw. And although it all sounds mighty complex, hard to follow even, we'll get a sort of distilled version, which then sits very nicely alongside your map. What I'm saying is that the `when` of it all is important, as it begins to point towards a much more comprehensible landscape and social history. It may predate our arrival on the scene; following the final departure of the last ice age, but on the greater scheme of things, not by so very much. Then we, humanity that is, came along and started to change things, but I'm going to argue that our lands above the waterheads are the least changed of all, where our human activity has been much less obvious in its effects on the landscape. This will start to take care of clue number two."

"Man alive, you've wasted no time in getting stuck into it, my friend."

"Well, it's a truly enjoyable and challenging project, that may have profound significance in the future. I'll press on, as I want to identify and wherever possible, name all The Spirit's myriad of tops and crags. Wouldn't go so far as to describe this as just creating a list, as I want to know more about average elevation, and how its structured across the Scottish landform. I also want for least a random selection, the meanings of the names, because that gives us a bit of a blast from the past. Again, quite detailed, but once the tops are lined up in the correct order, and their groupings identified, it will be a fairly simple picture."

I just let Ronald continue.

"I've kind of skipped the deep peat one for now, as I want to know more about habitat diversity and designation. There's some urgency with this, as I want to be able to know just about everything there is to know about the areas you`ve chosen. Putting your notes and pictures into the wider context will be ground-breaking stuff. That's where I`m at so far, and I`m beginning to be more-ready and better prepared for your, what shall we call it, fieldwork? Or hill-work, perhaps?"

Ordering more coffee, and enjoying its undoubted quality, I felt we were in the right place for this, sitting on seats and at a table made by the late great Tim Stead, whose designs grew from the very character of the wood itself, from what nature had made. But I was brought back from this indulgent thought, by Ronald.

"Well that's about it, for now - more about thoughts and directions than facts at this stage, I`m afraid. I hear you`ve had a brush with an attempt on your life? Serious stuff, any ideas who or what, and will you be discouraged?"

"No discouragement whatever Ronald, in fact, if anything it`s stiffened my resolve; my determination to succeed, and from that to be able to report back accordingly to The Spirit. No, I haven't a clue who it was who torched me out of my tent. I was wondering with some alarm about Liz`s brother-in-law Jamie because he`s implacably opposed to my, our quest. To make matters a whole lot worse, he attacked me quite violently at Liz`s cousin`s wedding. But I rather think he was a bit pissed at the time. Mind you; he was then admitted to a psychiatric hospital in Perth on the way home, and was too busy discharging himself and getting back to his work when the torching took place. Anyway, there`s no way he could have got up there in the middle of the night with a can of paraffin, and then got clean away. I know he likes shooting and killing things on the moors, but not after dark. He`s more-or-less off the list, for now."

If not Jamie, then who or what had sought so forcefully to dislodge me from my precarious path, I asked within my mind time after time, during a restless night back in Peebles? Was it fair to both Liz and Ronald to continue a course that might harbour more danger yet? And what was it all for; some rather abstract indulgence for my curiosity or the need for change? The questions piled in one upon the other, the dark thoughts conspired.

The sound of a text arriving on my phone in the wee hours distracted me from my dire imaginings, and I saw that it was from Liz. It read quite simply, "I love you Pandy," followed by three capital Xs. My train of thought changed to something altogether more optimistic. She, of all people, knew me best; five years together had created a strong bond between us. Her short nocturnal message gave the direction and renewed my resolve to go on. Liz knew how I would react and respond to danger, and clearly had confidence in my abilities, where mine had faltered. Thinking of how Ronald was already beginning to make sense of my observations, and where we might be going with this quest, helped to re-start my spirit of discovery. In these two, I knew I had sound allies who both wanted to see the finished result, whatever it might be. They were, I thought, on parallel but very different paths in which my best interests prevailed.

After the fire, I'd to re-organise my gear. So before coming back up to Liz's I looked closely at what I'd lost, what I still had, how compromises could be made, I worked out from this exercise what, if any, would need replacing. Another visit to that shop in Rose Street ensued.

Knowing from the outset that this mission would involve me in a lot of travel, and much of it by train, I set out to make these journeys as productive as possible. Heading for Forsinard, I'd taken a few well-selected guides to the Flow Country, to help focus on where I was bound: Knockfinn Heights.

That book which I'd bought in what now seemed like an age ago in Inverness Station also came to hand, though it was already looking a bit battered and stained. But I read eagerly about the evidence or belief in another dimension to the landscape; one which couldn't be defined by human knowledge alone. It most certainly set me thinking that if the ancients, our ancestors, had been attuned in some way to this other world of faery beings or whatever they chose to call them, then who are we to deny this possibility. Are we any wiser today, or any more attuned to nature than those who lived, and out of necessity interacted more fully with the natural world around them?

As the train clicked along with coast and hill rolling past, I found myself caught up in something so much more human and tantalising than the merely philosophical. The most pressing belief for me right now, is a conviction that The Spirit was real, had given me something very real to do, and that there was a genuine urgency in it. A strange mix of experience, what I was reading in the book, what I already knew or understood, and a genuine openness seemed to be coming together to create an honest conviction in the compelling wisdom bound-up in the Seven Signs.

It was clear from the map I was studying as the countryside rolled by that there was something most unusual, special indeed, in this Flow Country bog on Knockfinn Heights. It had few contour lines, and they were spaced well apart, so it must be almost flat. It did have the odd spot height and a trig point, so it was not totally featureless. To get to it would mean going up to this elevated area, so in a sense, it was on top of the hill. And it had more open water in the form of lochans and pools than I'd ever seen before in one place. To crown it all, it straddled the line of the watershed. It was almost as if the water couldn't make up its mind which way to go. Just looking at the map was raising my sense of anticipation.

With the addition to this watery picture, of all the information gleaned from guides and booklets, it was becoming clear that this Flow, as it was called, was very special indeed. Ronald would make even more sense of all of it when I sent him my notes and photos. He could then marry this up with all he'd discover in his researches.

When the train finally came to a halt in Forsinard, after a quick visit to the information centre, I used the remaining daylight to walk to my eco-rich destination, and camp for the night.

A whole day was then spent exploring and simply experiencing the Knockfinn Heights, with dozens of photos taken to try and make some king of visual record. These would add to the many images that would be available on-line, but also act as a very tangible reminder of the experience and the place. The spirit had devoted one of his clues to irreplaceable deep peat and Flow; was this I wondered, what he had in mind? There now seemed no doubt about it. It was with a sense of reverence that in my splendid solitude I gently trod the seemingly elastic surface vegetation, which somehow floated on top of the water-laden bog. Although I could see my image reflected on the surfaces of the pools, I could also look deeper into at least something of their mystery. As an occasional light breeze drifted across the landscape, the ripples on each successive pool gave back the dancing light of sun, sky, and puffy cloud. The whole scene was captivating.

Whereas my earlier outing in the Borders had been framed so well by the hills and adjacent valleys, in this one, it was the wide skies that seemed so distinctive. Distance was harder to judge from my more subtly elevated vantage, and I ventured, that there is indeed something unique about this countryside. The flowing horizon was subtle, more-gentle, and with few dramatic features to hold the eye. But the totality of it was inspiring; it wasn't difficult to see why the entire conservation movement had taken this place, and its ilk elsewhere in Scotland, to its heart, and now sought to protect it for its extraordinarily special wildlife value.

Beneath the immense dome of the sky, my human presence seemed small, but I felt a profound interaction with the landscape around me, as I meant to celebrate in some way, its profoundly rich character.

One incongruous feature in the landscape which I found it hard to ignore was a large amount of commercial forestry. Having read up on it, I also knew that this change had come about resulting from the fiscal regime which enabled the rich to manage their tax affairs to their advantage while destroying valuable habitats. It worked well for them on the one hand and was an environmental disaster on the other. Thankfully things were changing for the good. The tax breaks were no longer as attractive for those wealthy individuals, coming mainly from the south-east of England.

They had discovered that the value of the peat-bog they'd been bent on destroying was now being celebrated not for its purely financial possibilities, but rather, for its eco-value. The environmental heavyweights had moved in armed with chainsaws and the means to raise the water table once more. I found myself warming to this gradual and wholly positive transformation, though did reckon that Jamie and his ilk would be scunnered that the tables were turning.

In the evening, I sent Ronald as much as I possibly could of the whole immersion in delight. Some of it I stored on The Cloud and smiled warmly as it occurred how fitting that was in this place. The evening light was transforming the great dome of everything within the wide horizon into a spread of pink promise. Sleep came easily in the short period of darkness, and the following day continued the utterly engrossing exploration of this special place. A very long way from the everyday.

Chapter Eleven

My trance-like state was disturbed by a soft but incongruous sound coming from over my left shoulder. Before I could look around to investigate, I received a sudden blow to the back of my head which almost knocked me senseless. This was followed by being grabbed around the neck by someone who I immediately imagined was fit and strong. Struggling to my feet, I realised I'd must fight back with all the strength I could give it. Swinging a punch at my assailant, I caught him a good blow on the side of his head.

"What the fuck you up to?" I yelled.

There was no response, just an attempt to re-tighten the arm-hold that he had on my neck. I found I could shift some of my weight onto my left foot, and so use the rest to give him a right kick with my hard-soled boot which connected firmly with his knee. We then wrestled to the ground and rolled around amongst the heather and moor grasses; both grunting between brief spells of heavy breathing. He still said nothing by way of any explanation but seemed intent on doing me as much damage as he could.

We exchanged blows to head and chest, grabbed whatever we could of the other, arms, head-locks, hair, I even made a bold attempt to get hold of his balls. One of my kicks did get him in the stomach, but one of his caught me in the thigh. His footwear may have been lighter than mine, and I reckoned he was a bit shorter, but his apparent strength and fitness more than made up for that. He had got the advantage in this brutal and sudden assault.

As we rolled and struggled, we drifted nearer to one of the lochans and fell into the dark peat-stained waters with a dull splash. Realising that I was more underwater than was going to do me any good, I mustered all my strength and wits, and just managed to swing a punch that connected firmly with his nose. This must have taken him by surprise, as he smartly loosened his grip on me, and I got another punch which hit him just above his left eye. Blood was starting to show from the first blow.

There was no chance, and even less point now, in trying to reason with him. He grabbed my throat with both hands and was clearly intending that I should drown. Grabbing a lungful of air before I was submerged in the murky waters, I realised that there was no foothold to be had, for these peat pools are bottomless. As I went down, I saw a glimpse of his glaring brown eyes, red weather-beaten complexion, and greying red hair. But that was indeed a brief glimpse, for I soon realised that I was in grave danger.

Keeping his grip on my neck, the only saving grace was that the slimy water was preventing him from squeezing enough to choke me. We continued to writhe and flail. My hands and arms and his feet being the focus of the action.

`Need to go back to schoolboy tactics I reckoned, in which there are no real rules, so wrenching my head round far enough to bite him hard on the arm - his mistake in not wearing a long-sleeved garment. Realising that I couldn`t hold my breath for much longer, I grabbed his clothing pulled him closer to me, and brought my right knee up as hard as I possibly could, into his groin.

This had the desired effect, as he groaned in agony, and let go of me, so I surfaced, spat out the mouthful brown sludge that I`d taken in on the way up, and took in a few rapid gasps of breath.

This seemed to give a brief respite in the assault, so I struggled away from him, to leave him still breathless from the kneeing I`d inflicted. I swam over to the bank but realised it wasn't at all firm. It was just a few clumps of vegetation and peat overhanging the water. I'd have to pull myself out, and onto that, I quickly realised. So, not even looking back to see where he was, I took as firm a grip as I possibly could on a couple of clumps that looked likely, hauled myself up a bit, and so got a bit more of my body clear of that water. Still holding on firmly, I managed to swing my body around, and bring my legs up a bit. From this position, I somehow got my right leg out of the water. With a supreme effort and with no stronger purchase that what my hands could hold onto, and pray that that heather was good healthy stuff, I swung it up onto the bank in a place where there was a little less of the vegetation. I got enough of a toe hold on that, to pull my other leg up beside it, and with my centre of gravity now more on the bank such as it was, than in the water, I rolled over and found myself once more on what would have to pass as terra-firma.

No time to ponder on my apparent good fortune, though, as my assailant was only just behind me. I turned quickly, to where he was trying to get out of the water in much the same way as I had. He`d some sort of grip on the heather, so I stamped my boots on each of his fists. At this point, I heard the first words that he uttered. But they were just a succession of oaths and invective aimed very much at me. I realised that for the first time in my life, I was in a situation where it's him or me. He had had the earlier advantage, now that opportunity was mine; I intended to use it to full effect. So, I slumped to my knees where he was now once again trying to get himself out of the water, trying to regain some hold on the heather, but my boot work on his hand had clearly had a real impact. With the second one, on his right hand, I had twisted my boot a couple of times. Blood was now coming from his knuckles, and the damage to his nose was still evident, with the blood mingling with the brown peat stained water, was streaking down his face.

I grabbed his hair, leant forward a bit while shoving my legs out behind me to keep my balance, and forced his head under the water. He writhed and flailed for a while. I wondered how long it would take a fit man to drown because I had every intention of drowning him. I would face the consequences later when I'd at least be alive.

After what seemed like ages, he stopped fighting and moving. So, I gave is head one more shove, and got up on my feet. The adrenalin must still have been pumping. Taking my bearings, and remembering from the map, that there were paths or moor tracks and some habitation called The Glutt to the northeast, I quickly worked out the direction I must go. Swinging my rucksack on my back, I almost sprinted across the heather and veered around all the many lochans that I encountered.

The sound of a quad bike roaring down the hill behind, filled me with dismay, as I clearly hadn't drowned him after all. No time to ponder that one, I just redoubled my efforts; escape was the only way. Utterly without scruples, he caught me enough of a glancing blow by one of the front wheels to send me head-first into the heather. Before I could catch my wind, he was on top of me, bound my hands and feet with tape, and loaded me onto the back of the machine.

The building I found myself coming to in must have been a kind of venison store or larder. My grim cell had wooden slats floor to ceiling on three sides, and a solid door, which I found to be locked from the outside, on the fourth. Above my head, the carcass of a deer hung from a hook; not very promising company at all. Nothing else for it than to find a way of breaking out of this morgue. After much painful arm squirming, I managed to liberate my hands form the grip of the tape, and then remove it from my legs too; a first, if agonising, step towards freedom.

With no tools or levers provided for this rare eventuality of being imprisoned with a rancid very dead deer, a quick survey of the slats revealed that a few were perhaps less robust than the others. Taking one of my boots off, I wedged it between the weakest looking adjoining slats and twisted with every ounce of strength that was left in me. It gave a slight cracking sound. Twisting the other way this time, it cracked some more. After about five minutes of this frenzied assault on the woodwork, one of the slats finally split. Grabbing the two pieces of wood which were each slotted into grooves on the frame on either side, I pulled them free. Putting my boot back on, I used the pair of new-found levers to break some more adjoining slats and created a hole big enough to wriggle through, landing in an undignified heap on the ground outside. Looking around, I found that my assailant had dumped my rucksack in some rushes growing beside the track leading up to the structure.

The distant sound of a vehicle approaching raised my fears to a crescendo; I was convinced he was coming back to get me and finish me off. An image raced through my head of me joining what was left of the deer and would be found, who knew when, hanging, rotting, from the other hook. Darting into the shadows of an adjoining shed, I waited anxiously.

A little red van driven by the postman came around the bend and pulled up in the yard. He got out, to go over to the Lodge, and without a further thought, I grabbed my bag and landed myself in the passenger seat.

When he returned, he instantly demanded to know what I thought I was doing. "I cannot carry passengers in the van, that's the company rules, pal."

"Listen, you've got to get me out of here, I've been half drowned by some madman, who then ran me down with his quad bike, knocked me out and then locked me in that venison larder over there. Rules or no, I appeal for your help, now."

There was a brief silence as it was clear he was trying to weigh up the situation, and the apparent plight of his uninvited passenger. About to speak with a new plea to him, he interrupted my hurried plan, and by saying rather cautiously "OK, I suppose. What you've said sounds reasonably convincing, and I did see a lunatic on a quad bike a few miles back. Right, but keep your head down. Here put your bag in the back, and I'll get you as far as I can.

"Man, am I grateful to you for this." I gasped

He heard more of my story, as we bumped along the track, and he got me to a house at a crossroads. There, he handed me over to a surly looking man who said he was heading a bit nearer to town, and although he never gave lifts to hitchers, was glad to accept Rab the postie's request. The escape became a bit of a blur, but I seemed to be passed from one rescuer to another, before eventually being left with a woman called Mags Gunn, domestic supervisor in an oversized shooting lodge. She was happy it seemed, to have some company for a few hours as the place had no guests at the time. Duly fed and watered, I was given the space and facilities to get cleaned and dried out, and a nap at the end of it came as a welcome release.

When I did wake, in the evening, I found that one of my legs was in severe pain, and I feared had suffered some internal damage in the attack.

"Not a problem," said Mags. "I`ll take you over to the minor injuries service at our local hospital in Thurso. Well, I do hope it is a minor injury, as the alternative would be A & E much further away, in Wick. Then, all being well you can come back here for the night. Anyone you want to contact first, though?"

"Yes, I`ll phone my partner Liz, but she might be a bit alarmed to hear of another incident so soon after the first. I wonder could you also put the word around your scattered neighbourhood about this lunatic on a quad bike. Gamekeepers and stalkers are usually observant folks. A description, or even discovering who`s machine he may have nicked would be good."

"Yes, glad to help."

While I phoned Liz on the guest telephone, Mags must have used another one to do some phoning around. Liz was understandably concerned. The fact that I could report that I`d sent Ronald all the notes, and photos before the attack, didn`t placate her fears one bit.

"I`ll be up to meet you in Inverness at the very least, once you've decided when you`re coming back to civilisation and safety. Phone me back soon."

Mags loaded me into a big Land Rover and took me as she`d said she would to the hospital. "Hello Mags, what have you got for us this time?". Greeted our arrival. I left it her to do some of the explaining.

"Right we`ll check you out, and do what we can Andy, and given what's happened, the Police will need to be informed. I`ll give them a call shortly;" the well-uniformed nurse announced. He was fresh-faced, middle-aged, and above all very friendly. Mags found a comfortable seat and settled down to a magazine, where a cup of tea somehow appeared for her.

He took all the details he needed and ushered me through to a sort of consulting room. There, he inspected me thoroughly; "Given the going over you have had, we need to be sure of all possibilities."

Although I said it was my leg that was the real problem, he left nothing to chance. In the end, he summarised his findings with, "Well, you'll be pleased to know nothing's broken, and unlikely to be any lasting damage anywhere. Can see that you've got a bad sprain and bruising on your leg, so I'll put a Tubi dressing on it to give it some real support for now. And I'd best give you a tetanus jag too."

After these nursing attentions, had been done, a couple of inquisitive Police appeared around the door. Thanking the nurse for his thorough attention, I was taken through to an empty day-room, where once again, the usual details were taken down, for the record. My account of what had happened was as thorough as I could usefully make it. On referring to my earlier arson attack down in the Borders area, I added that this time I had a description of my assailant to offer. "Age, perhaps mid to late forties, height about five-five, glaring brown eyes, red weather-beat complexion and greying red hair. He was wearing sort of outdoor gear, but the camouflage variety. Just possible there's a gamekeeper sort of connection too, I added. That's about all I can remember."

They thanked me, and one asked, "Eh, what were you doing up on Knockfinn Heights anyway? Are you a birdwatcher or something?"

"More of a something really. Was exploring the nature and character of the landscape for a personal and very harmless project I'm doing."

"OK, thanks. Oh, by the way, there's been a report of a quad bike being stolen from around Kinbrace area yesterday, and it was found near Dunbeath a wee while ago this evening. Given what you've told us, we'll get that checked out for fingerprints. We'll also be in touch with our colleagues in the Scottish Borders, as these two incidents might be related, or linked. If they are, someone sure as hell has it in for you, big style."

Back at the lodge, Mags fed me once more and told me that she had to go down to Inverness next day for some supplies, so could give me a lift, if I wanted to go south again.

"I'd appreciate that very much. I've done what I came up here for, so it is indeed time to go home."

"You certainly got more than you bargained for Andy, but just to reassure you, these kinds of events are very rare indeed, up here."

Chapter Twelve

Mags had been hugely generous, and helped me through the aftermath of the latest ordeal, so stepping out of her employer's big comfortable vehicle at Inverness station, I thanked her heartily for all that she'd done. We exchanged the sincerely meant vows to keep in touch, and she was gone; on her quest to stock up the larder or whatever the lodge needed in large quantities at that time.

With perhaps half an hour before Liz's train was due, I phoned round a couple of hotels, and got us booked into a central one that promised fine views of the river. I also booked us a meal in a nearby restaurant. We would experience Inverness in restrained but comfortable style.

As I saw the train approaching I could see the ticket barriers were open, so just breezed onto the platform and we could welcome and embrace the minute she stepped down. We were both it seemed equally pleased to see the other.

Hotel first, get freshened up, best clothes available, and we were off to the restaurant, where the fine meal, wine and chat were equal partners. Quick walk up the river to Ness Islands, where we took a little of the evening air, and then back to the hotel.

There we made love gently because my injuries, or so Liz assured me, and in that warm bliss after the event, we just lay and chatted affectionately.

Waiting for me on our return to Lauderdale Street, was an envelope written in Archie's distinctive handwriting with my name on it, and it was lying on top of my tray in the kitchen. Unable to recall any such missive from him ever before, and sitting here in Liz's flat, it intrigued me, especially given his mischievous streak. But it also raised a little anxiety, because the strain and division within in his family. Only one thing to do, and that was open it.

Liz had made some coffee for us almost as soon as we got out of the taxi from the station, so with a mug at my elbow, and the envelope in hand, I sat down, to discover the content; whatever it may be.

Inside, was a handwritten note inviting me to lunch in his club on Friday. He added, that Jamie would be there also.

`Jesus, more questions than answers in this one`, was the very first thought that launched itself at me. To say it put me in a panic, might be just a minor overstatement, but I sure as hell was concerned. Telling myself to think straight, it occurred that this gathering of the three of us, would take place in neutral, and highly civilised surroundings. Archie had never appeared to me to be in any way malicious, given to mischief perhaps, but never apparently out to cause harm. This thought, calmed me a little.

When Liz came back into the kitchen, apparently having had a shower, I felt I should bring her into the picture straight away.

"Your Dad, has just sent me a note inviting me to lunch, along with Jamie on Friday. What do you make of that, my love?"

"Hm, I did wonder what was in that envelope that he asked me to deliver to you. What is the old bugger up to this time, I wonder?"

"I`m wondering too, and filled with a bit of, shall we say, foreboding? No doubt he`ll have some purpose in mind."

"Well, firstly, are you going to go, and secondly, I`ll try and suss-out very discreetly if Mum knows anything about it. I`m certainly not going to mention it to Hermione. But Dad can be a cunning one, and you can bet that this is not just a social thing to while away a lunchtime. Where did you say he`s taking you?"

"His Club. I guess the good thing about that is its formal, and probably has an air of respectability about it. Hopefully that will set the scene a wee bit."

"Some homecoming Pandy, this'll have taken your mind off the happenings of the last few days, for sure."
"Do you think my best work clothes will be suitable for the occasion, or should I go down the road and collect my suit?"
"No, I think what you have here will be fine, and I don't mind polishing your shoes for you."
"Right now, I'm knackered, so I'm going to have a nap, and I mean a nap, before I head for a tutorial I need to do later this afternoon. What are you going to do?"
A bit of shut-eye sounds very good, then I'll go through the routine of sorting my stuff. Meeting with Ronald is on the cards for tomorrow."
Got an idea of making us something beef-based for dinner, so leave all that to me."
"Oh, that'll be great thank you, I'd like that. You can be a bit of a dab-hand at this cooking business, when the mood takes you."
For once, I arrived at the usual meeting place a bit before Ronald. "Sorry I'm late;" he announced twenty minutes later. "I'd an article about Forest Schools to finish for the Times Ed Supp. Always like to stir things up a bit there. You've been in the wars, yet again, from what you said in your last email."
"Sure have, no lasting damage, surprisingly, because the bugger was most certainly out to eliminate me. Got a good description of him though, to add to the growing Police files. There was something faintly familiar about him, but I just can't pin it down at all. Hasn't put me off the quest in the slightest, I must stress. You and I are still in business together on this very fine eco-mission. I'm going to go back up to Rhidorroch within the next couple of weeks, so I do hope to catch up with The Spirit, for a re-charge, if nothing else."
"Don't think you need too much re-charging, my friend, as you seem pretty up-beat and motivated already. But I know what you mean."

Four hours, three coffees, two buns and one distracting phone call each later, we had brought as much of the project as was humanly possible up to date. The reports I'd filed with Ronald, had been very helpful and perceptive, he assured me.

"And I found that they were a perfect fit alongside the research I've done. In fact, they shone a lot of clear light on all the relevant citations and designation docs, which could otherwise sometimes appear as rather bland enviro-speak. The official story about a bit of landscape may be technically accurate, but it lacks soul. You've been righting that imbalance very well - whether you know it or not."

"Well that is good to know, as there's a stark contrast between getting almost stoned on the atunement to landscape one day, and having brutal assault on your life the next. The one rather knocks the stuffing out of the other, for a day or three at least. It rather loses its direction and feeling on the way. It's very reassuring to hear from you that this is working despite it all."

"If you can keep going with your observations and feelings about what you are experiencing or immersing yourself in, no pun intended, I assure you Andy, then I can make perfect sense of it. And you have my word, that I'll have a firm hold on the spirit of place; on what you are describing so well."

"Here's a strange one though Andy. Was at a land management seminar the other day, and was chatting over coffee to a guy I kind of know who's in the Estate and Land crowd, or whatever it's called, so I took the opportunity to sound him out on how militant they are. Raised an eyebrow, did that one, but I light heartedly pressed him on how far he thought some of the gang would go to maintain the status quo, and on the issues like defending traditional and often secretive ownership. Although he ducked it really, he did say that there was possibly a fanatical fringe with its` hangers-on. We'd to break off the conservation there unfortunately, as the next session was called. Pity, as I'd like to have fished around a wee bit more. A very telling confession, if that's what it was, I'd say though."

"But back to the issues in hand for today, Andy."

"The need to be very organised with all the info we are gathering goes without saying, so I'm structuring it around a chart I've devised. I know it sounds far too bloody formal, but it's working for me. Main things I'm listing are location and distance along the Watershed, and all the different forms of local, Scottish, UK, European, and global environmental designations. These give the reason why an area, large or small, is important, who says so, for what reason, along with something of its status."

Ronald had my rapt attention, as it was making the suffering I'd endured, worth it.

"Although it's very early days, I can already say with confidence, that the lands above the waterheads are extraordinarily special, and almost twice as well designated or protected as the rest of Scotland. Did a wee exercise the other day to try and compare our very lengthy geographic feature with a couple of others on a similar scale, and on the simple criterion of designation and protection, ours is vastly more eco-significant; probably about twice as protected as the rest. Each site is a dot, or larger blob on my map. What we need to focus on in due course, is joining up the dots. When you meet The Spirit, you'll know that somehow, he got it uncannily right, he wasn't fantasising in any way. His knowledge and understanding of the very soul of Scottish landscape is profound, probably unique."

Chapter Thirteen

The exterior of Archie's club in Abercromby Place, exuded good order and confidence, which blended with the same assertion as the rest of the street. Beyond that, the only evidence showing of the purpose of this doorway, was a modest brass plaque above a small entry-phone.
Any sense of nervousness was eased slightly, as I saw Jamie heading towards the same doorway from the opposite direction; his normal cock-sure gait was gone.
"Hello Jamie, well I wonder what this event's about, have you any idea?" I ventured, to break the ice.
"None, I'd doubts about coming in the first place, as things have changed."
"Well, let's go in, and we'll see what Archie has in store for us, shall we?"
Crossing the threshold, having ushered Jamie in ahead of me, we were enveloped in brass, glass, mahogany, and rich blue. Clearly the door-man had been briefed, as he greeted us with, "So which of you is Andy, and who answers to Jamie?"
This informality was quite unexpected, and further served to put me, at least, more at ease. I took the initiative of introducing us, and that was the cue.
"This way please, Archie, eh, Mr Ferguson, is ready to welcome you to the Abercromby Club, and to lunch."
Entering the dining room was like continuing a journey through a time warp; decor, furnishings, formal table settings, and staff in suitable uniforms, all contributed to an atmosphere which seemed to fit a stereotype, only as seen on the movies for most of us. Archie stood up to greet us.
"Jamie, lovely to see you, and so glad you could make it;" as he shook his hand in a firm and convivial manner.

"Thank you for inviting me sir;" came Jamie's overly formal, but clearly nervous response.

"And Andy, I'm so pleased to welcome you, and delighted that you too could make it too. Here, please sit down, and make yourselves comfortable. Well, you've both been in the wars from what I hear, but we are not here to re-run these in any way, let me assure you."

Dear God, that's a relief, I sighed inwardly. Now just bloody well relax, man.

A waiter appeared with the menus, which we studied briefly, in silence. "Now have whatever you would like gents, I can vouch for all of it. Though I confess that I struggle with having the full three courses at this time of day, myself. Have whatever takes your fancy though. Please."

Decided to break the ice, "I'd like the fish please Archie, and if that's OK, I'll see how I'm fixed for a sweet afterwards."

"That's grand;" as Archie nodded to the waiter. "Now Jamie, it's your turn."

"I'll have the venison please, eh, Archie. And perhaps also wait to see about another course later."

"Excellent." Looking up to the waiter he also ordered the fish. "We'll have my usual red to go with the venison, Bert, and the white that you know I like, for the fish." Closing the menus, the waiter took them from us and departed with a formal nod of the head.

"Well I've now heard from the various tradesmen about the improvements at the Home Farm, so it should be very much ready for us in the summer. Andy, I do hope you'll join us this year, and that you'll convince Elizabeth that she simply must be part of the house party. I'm sure that if you work your socks off to help get her exhibition ready, at least one week for the two of you together at Spurryhillock would be possible."

"I'd love to thanks Archie, and very much hope that it all works out. I've heard so much about the place over the years, that it would indeed be nice to see it, and to discover more of that area. Haven't been to that part of Scotland very often, I must say."

Jamie, meanwhile had been sitting quietly, fidgeting a bit and I could see that his shoulders were not as straight as normal. But how was I to regard him today? he hadn't changed in my estimation; once a pillock, always a pillock. Well in this case anyway; contrary to my normal optimistic view of the people I met. Decided to just see how things panned out.

The waiter reappeared with the food, so Archie invited us to tuck-in.

"Do hope things are picking up for you Jamie. All very unsettling for everyone. The girls and Hermione are fine for now. How are you and the dogs coping together over in Aberlady?"

"Oh, I guess we are all right. The house is a bit empty, but I keep it tidy. Work has been busy with that project up near Loch Rannoch to deal with. You'll know General Farquharson-Whamond, I'm sure? He works for a firm of solicitors in Drummond Place, I believe. Confess that we just call him Rannoch, after the name of his estate. Trying to get it all ready for his retirement from the city life."

"Oh yes, there was a time when we had the odd game of golf together."

"I'd like to think that things will be, what shall I say, sufficiently sorted out Jamie, for you to join us all at the Home Farm too, but I imagine we'll just need to see how it works out, won't we."

"Eh, yes. I believe so."

"Now, are you enjoying your fish and venison? It is good, isn't it. And hopefully you find that the wine is just right in each case. I do think it's important to get these things right. Did I hear Elizabeth say that you come from Galloway, Newton Stewart, I think, Andy? Lovely area, though perhaps a few too many spruce trees for my liking. Good fishing in the River Cree, or there certainly used to be. And some of the hill lochs have good fish to be had too. Sorry, I'm rambling."

"Yes, Galloway born and bred. I do miss it sometimes, but my life there wasn`t crowned with success, having perhaps left school a bit early. But there`s not much you can do with the frustrations of hind-sight, now is there? Anyway, my life is well and truly up here with Liz now. My folks are still there, and still working. I`m afraid my mother may be at least partly responsible for some of those trees you aren`t so keen on, as she works for the Forestry Commission."

"Oh well, I very much doubt if she actually planted any of them herself;" at which Archie had a good chuckle at his wee joke. "So, Andy, that's your job and your career behind you, and you are currently tramping the hills on some great environmental mission, I gather. How`s that coming along? Are you enjoying it, and is it challenging enough for you?"

"Thoroughly enjoying it thanks, an immensely rewarding venture, where I`m discovering much more than I ever imagined I would. Had a couple of wee incidents, but have survived unscathed, which if anything has just redoubled my determination to do what I set out to do, and get all the pleasure that goes along with this."

As I said all this, I kept an eye on Jamie, to see what reaction he would have. Had no intention of antagonising him, but if there was anything, I reckoned it would register in some way. Whilst there was perhaps a reaction, in that his shoulders straightened briefly, his brows knitted momentarily, and he gave a kind of shiver, it was not a strong reaction. This puzzled me given all that he had said and done previously. But perhaps he was for now at any rate, more beaten than had seemed possible.

"You call it a venture Andy, tell me more please, if you like. What are you aiming to achieve?"

Well here goes, I thought. "You`ll know that I`ve a great interest in environmental matters, and have had for many years. It`s a mixture of getting out and just enjoying the outdoors for what it is of course, but I`ve done a bit of campaigning too. Everything is not entirely well with the way we exercise our stewardship of our environment, and in my view and that of many others like me; it needs to improve significantly." Picking my words carefully, I then went on to divert away from the controversial. Archie was probably old-school in these matters, so I didn`t want to offend; being his guest for a good lunch did carry obligation.

He then cut in with something that really filled me with some amazement. "Oh, I agree on some, indeed much of what you say. As part of my share of good works, and yes, a bit of conscience perhaps, I act as legal advisor to one of the major Scottish environmental organisations. They do quite a bit of campaigning at the more motivated end of the spectrum, but I`m very glad to freely give my time and legal counsel. Also, advise on their constitutional and staffing matters. You probably don`t know about this Jamie. I kind of keep it low profile, not because it presents me with any image problem, but it suits them: no, I`m not going to name the organisation. Sorry."

Jamie was sitting silently through all this shaking his head in slow motion, and playing with a piece of venison at the end of his fork.

"Do continue Andy, please, I`ve interrupted you."

"No problem, and I do think you are to be admired for this voluntary and very valuable role that you play, for whatever organisation it is Archie. There's not a great deal more to add really, other than that I`m on what I would call a quest which was entrusted to me by a mystical character I met in an area called Rhidorroch. He gave me a note of what he called the Seven Signs of Enduring and Continuous Wildness, I can email them to you if you like, as they're still a bit of an environmental conundrum. They concern the very special landscape qualities of a feature that he called the lands above the waterheads. It is in fact the watershed of Scotland, our own version of what in The States they call their Great Divide. Reckon I`ve got the clues

unravelled, and a journalist friend helping me with the research, I just need to get out and enjoy gathering the evidence."
"Fascinating, a quest, on a possibly epic scale. But what do you plan to do with it when you have it all pulled together?"
"That, I do not know, at this stage. Will just need to see where we go from that. One thing I would add though is that not too many people know about this project, and I`d rather like to keep it that way for now, please."
"Not a problem with me Andy, you OK with that, Jamie?"
But he just gestured in a way that was non-committal.
"Right, time for some pudding I think. The sticky toffee pudding is quite superb, so shall we all just have that?" Without waiting for any answers, Archie beckoned the waiter, and ordered up accordingly. "Oh, and coffees to follow, Bert. Thanks."
"I`ll be fascinated to hear more of this project of yours Andy. When you feel the time`s right, of course."
"Now Jamie, we are being most rude, and leaving you out of this discussion. How are things at McDuff & Parker right now? I hope they are treating you well?"
"Oh, yes thanks, things are fine there. I've got a few good projects on the go with several our Estates, and hope to see them reap the benefits from various renewable energy projects. The usual battles and anti-this and anti-that brigade to contend with, but if we can be patient, I`m sure it will all come right for us, for them rather, in the end. Always a lot of traveling to be done, but being on my own right now means a little bit less of a rush. M & P was sounding me out for a new more senior post dealing with urban renewal on industrial wasteland, but I wasn`t so keen on that. Just said I was very happy with my current post. Anyway, it keeps me in, with some of the estates people, which I do enjoy."
"Jolly good, but don`t forget that a bit of ambition is no bad-thing in your field. I`ve seen chaps stagnate."

"I`d like to think I`m steering well clear of that pitfall, Archie. But thanks for the hint."

Archie had been spot on his assessment of the sticky toffee pudding, but I felt obliged to decline the offer of second helpings. Rounding the meal off with coffee, was a fitting conclusion.

"`Fraid I`ve a client to see at two-thirty boys, so we`ll need to call it a day. But let's repeat it sometime. Delighted to treat you both, and do not forget the open door at Spurryhillock Home Farm in August."

With that, we both thanked him in our respective ways.

Once outside, I commented to Jamie that he had been rather subdued, and hoped things would indeed work out OK in the end. I also added light-heartedly, that I rather hoped I`d can get on with my quest without any more incident.

To this he simply commented, or mumbled if truth be told. "It may be too late. Psychopath."

When he said this, I was preoccupied with getting my cycling gear on, as it had started to rain, so had only been half listening. It was only when I got up and over the hill, to where that tram had very nearly got me a few weeks earlier, that it dawned on me what he had said. "What the fuck did he mean by that remark?" I yelled at yet another tram.

Chapter Fourteen

In the short journey, back across the city to Lauderdale Street, I got thoroughly drenched. The waterproofs were no match for the deluge that had the roads running like rivers, the gutters turning into small lochs, and some of the drains working in reverse. Without ceremony, I chained my bike to the front gate. Liz must have seen me coming, for the door swung open as if by magic, as I stood on the mat creating a rapidly growing puddle in the porch. Any feeling of dampened spirits evaporated however, as I could hear our favourite piece of music being broadcast throughout the house from the CD player. The contrast between the weather just encountered, and the exquisite interplay between instruments in Bach`s Double Violin Concerto, was profound.
One simple gesture from Liz to stay on the doorstep was quickly followed by the arrival of a large dry towel. How strange, I thought, to be divesting myself of much of my clothing just inside the door, and to the emotional heights engendered in this great piece of music. No hurry, I thought, why rush the experience.
A washing basket then appeared, with no words needed from Liz to dictate its purpose. And so, by the end of the slow movement, I was standing in my boxers in her kitchen drying my hair, and all the rest.
"That, my love, was a unique and very moving experience. Thank you for your assistance in protecting the place from all the wet I could so easily have spread around the place."
"Coffee?"
"Yes, please, you must have read my thoughts."
Once dried, clothed, and having closed the front door, I sat down to enjoy the equally beautiful 3rd movement, that teases its

way to a very satisfactory and musically logical conclusion. At which point I had my first mouthful of coffee.

"Now that we've dealt with your arrival on-stage Andy, how did it go. I'll be utterly intrigued to hear. But just stand up first, take a turn or two, and I'll check that there's no evidence of any violence having taken place."

Doing as I was bid, and to her satisfaction, I then sat down once more. "Could we have Beethoven's Violin Concerto next? You like it, and it has special significance for me."

"Sure, just hang on a minute, then you can recount the lunchtime deeds."

When she returned, and the music was getting into its stride, I stood up, and ensured that we had a warm embrace first. Well, it was all very civilised as you can imagine in that club of his; all very refined to set the scene, I daresay. The food was top notch, or should I say, delicious. Archie ensured that there was no chance of a re-play of the earlier antics. Jamie was undoubtedly quite subdued. Archie was his usual warm and friendly self. He was especially interested to hear more about my quest, and within that, he told us something that had me kind of gob-smacked. I'd always put him down as very much an establishment old school kind of chap, and no harm in that really. But next he informs us that he's the honorary legal advisor to one of Scotland's top environmental campaigning organisations. Does it as his bit of good works he says, fully in support of it and all that strives to achieve, but in a low-profile kind of way for him. Bet you never knew that about your father?"

"I did not, but from what you've just said, he has risen a mile in my estimation and respect for him. But what about Jamie in all this?"

"He was rather quiet and didn't have much to contribute, he admitted that he'd had the offer of a move within McDuff & Parker, to urban regeneration of old industrial sites, but he turned that down. Archie didn't say as much, but it was clear he was unimpressed; no ambition was the implication. So thankfully, he didn't try to get us to kiss and make-up, he didn't have a go at Jamie for having really fucked things up in the family. But he did stress that the door at the Home Farm will be very open this summer, and that he really wants us all there, Elizabeth, I mean Liz. Mind you he did indicate to Jamie that for him things would need to be sorted out on his family circumstances first."

"What was it all about - really? Why had he got the two of you together in the first place?"

"Honestly do not know Liz. Whatever it was, it was not obvious. The only thing I can think of is that it was a very Archie sort of thing, and just knowing that he'd could get us together in what for Jamie and I was neutral territory, and with no punch ups, would be an achievement. Archie's a smart cookie, so it would be somewhere in that kind of tactic."

"Guess you must be right, but in an odd way, it seems a bit of an anti-climax, what you've just told me. Don't know what drama I expected, but it hasn't happened. On the positive side, it'll have moved things forward half an inch, without any tears. Mummy and Hermione know nothing of this, so we are best to leave it that way. Was that it then?"

"No, not quite; as we were about to go our separate ways I was a bit preoccupied at donning my cycling gear in the rain, but commented I was hopeful that I'd be able to get on with my quest without any more incident. I certainly meant it, and wasn't consciously fishing for anything, but his response in a very mumbled remark was that 'it may be too late', and then simply the word 'psychopath'. As I say I was busy getting ready for a cycle in the rain and it was a full ten minutes later that I realised what he'd said, and I have not got a clue what he meant by it. Can hardly go back and ask him. It was un-rehearsed and deliberate; he knows something and is either unwilling, or more likely, quite unable to put a stop to what he`s set in motion.

Chapter Fifteen

Standing bravely beneath the great white blades as they rotated inexorably above me, their plunging path seemed to bring each one frighteningly close, before it soared skywards once more and left me unharmed. But this was instantly followed by another then another, and another in an endless air-slicing rhythm. With each dive towards, and as rapid ascent away, from me, there was a whoosh that was loudest when directly above my head. It seemed to me that everyone should at least take the opportunity to experience this; whether for or against wind turbines, they would argue their case from a better position, of having had some direct experience of their action, at the very least.

The exploration that day took me on a rambling circuit of hill and moor, in a landscape that while carrying many marks of our current or earlier activities, stood wild and proud above the urban sprawl of the central belt. Although at the northern edge of these uplands, the Gargunnock Hills and their neighbours gave ready access to an experience of relative wildness for almost half the population of Scotland, which lived and laboured within the vista below.

To Stronend, on the other side of a feature with the evocative name of the Spout of Ballochleam, I struggled through rough, tough tussocks of vegetation and knee-challengingly uneven terrain, to reach a summit with a trig marker, which stood assertively proud above a precipitous drop on the other three sides. Although it was not the major purpose of this outing, I found myself drawn to the landscape history that opened a new chapter in front of me to the north and west. Recalling that I`d read somewhere of a time, not so far back in the shaping of Scotland as we know it, that the low line of hills between the upper reaches of a much more extensive Firth of Forth and what would have been the Firth of Lomond, were all that separated the salt water on each side. With just a bit more erosion of those hills, Scotland above the central belt would have become the Island of Highland or something of that ilk. Dabbling in imaginings of this land-forming era and possible consequences, had me in something of a day-dream. But I pulled myself into something a bit more recent, as I pondered the changes in land use and character in what had been, and still is in places, Flanders Moss. A whole day could so easily have been whiled away, appreciating the whole business of transition and change that lay there, right at my feet.

Returning in a roundabout sort of way to the other side of this little valley, I was startled as I unwittingly put up several loudly squawking grouse. Signs of some very early wildflowers were beginning to show, and amongst some of the grey lichen on a rock or two, I found tiny crimson buds, that looked just like match-heads. The contrast in colour was truly eye-catching.

Up on the moor, the peace was shattered by the noise of a roaring quad bike, carrying two men in battle dress, or so it seemed, with the one on the back carrying a shotgun. They stopped to ask me what I was doing up here, but avoiding any response to that; I asked them what they were doing? The reply was that they were shooting hares, as they carry ticks, which then transfer to the grouse, and ruin the precious field-sports. Realising that this conversation would go nowhere useful, I moved on, and peace gradually returned.

Ten minutes later a hare appeared some thirty yards away, or rather it saw me while sitting up on its hind legs in the heather, erect, stock still, and proud; the one that got away. Then I wondered, what rhymes with ticks? Answer: pricks. how crass, to believe that killing the hares served any useful purpose. Yes, pricks about sums up those guys or their employers. Bearing a frown, I sighed.

With the prospect of a couple of hours of warm sunshine left ahead of me, I headed for the ancient cairn on the top of Carleatheran, where yet more photos were taken, and notes were written up. Noisy hare shooters notwithstanding, it was a joy to record so many positive characteristics of this slice of hilly countryside, and its place in the wider landscapes.

Setting up camp in the early evening had that familiar satisfaction of routine combined with creating somewhere secure for the night.

As I cooked my dinner, I was taken once more with the distant views across the entire upper reaches of the Forth Valley and then following the meandering lines of the Firth towards the open sea. Frustratingly, the maps that I had with me didn't extend to the mountainous parts of The Trossachs, so it was left to my memory to try and work out which mountain and Ben were what, so I listed mentally, what I could. Ben Lomond, Ben More, Ben Vorlich, they marched with their near neighbours all the way around to the Ochil Hills, that seemed to drop so abruptly into the flatlands beside the Forth estuary. Further round, I could just make out the Forth Bridges, and even a hint of the Pentland Hills. My dinner was almost cold by the time I stopped this mountain watching, and as I ate the tepid offering, I did wonder how much of what I was looking at would be picked out on the great line on the map that I'd drawn just a couple of weeks back. But answering that would be for another day.

The sounds of light rain overnight re-affirmed the value of a good tent and gave special meaning to the camping experience; atmosphere.

Chapter Sixteen

The experience of re-enjoying that superb vista across the Forth Valley in the morning light was wiped out in an instant, as a dull, heavy blow on the back of my head, sent my gaze in a wide rapid arc across the sky.

Darkness.

Crawling in agony, I somehow managed to move upwards from my precarious position on the brink of a long steep drop, that would have seen me fall many hundreds of feet, had I not miraculously stopped very abruptly on this ledge. Not sure how long I'd lain unconscious there, and uncertain about the extent of any injuries, my progress was tortuously slow. The only thing of which I was certain, was that I must get myself back up to the top of the cliff in one piece. Every move was cautious, painful, and demanded a good foot or handhold; preferably both.

Eventually creeping on all fours over the rim, I lay in the heather, and gasped with every emotion pumping through me; relief, disbelief, and rage; I just needed to convince myself that I was not dead, that I'd somehow survived the horror of being thrown over a cliff face.

Once I'd gathered whatever was left of my wits, and to my surprise, finding my rucksack intact in the long heather over in the direction of the turbines, my thoughts turned to escape. A place of safety was my number one priority now, lest whoever had done this, should return to finish the job more effectively.

Managing somehow, to stand up, I detached my walking poles from the side of the rucksack and hobbled in the general direction of the car some four miles away over very rough terrain. Despite the walking poles, I was in real pain as I took several tumbles which only served to add to the severity of it. Thankfully, however, the route I'd instinctively chosen took me ever further away from that ghastly crag.

There was no sign of anyone anywhere; I felt very alone, yet thankful that my assailant did not appear to be coming back.

After I know not how long my route finally joined a track, which it was clear, and led past a farmhouse, across a bridge and to the car park.

"Is this your car Sir?" the smaller of the two Policemen, demanded to know.

"Bloody hell yes, but what in the name of fuck has happened to it?" In dismay, I surveyed the broken windscreen and slashed tyres.

"Yes, it does seem to have been damaged deliberately, but I must caution you, that you are under arrest."

Dumbfounded and utterly speechless, I couldn't make any sense whatever of what was happening to me, I felt weak with confusion.

"You'll have to come with us, right now;" and to cap it all, they the cautioned me.

"B, but why, what am I supposed to have done? Jesus Christ, I've just been half murdered up there on that hilltop. I was thrown over the crag, in a determined effort by some bastard to kill me. So why are you arresting me? There's some murdering madman out there that you should be combing the countryside for."

"That's as may be. We've had a report, and we are acting on it, so it would be better if you came quietly with us now, away from all these people;" the taller of the two said as he gestured to the gathering crowd in the car park.

Jesus, the bastard must have got in there first, not just one, but several steps ahead of me; I`m up against a very clever and cynical madman, I groaned to myself. Not only are the Police failing miserably in their duty to catch him, but now they`re turning on me, on some miserable spurious basis too. If I do survive, it will be an out and out miracle.

"We`ll get your vehicle towed to safety;" I was then ordered to get in the rear door of the Police car.

As I sat in the back of the Police car, with the larger one sitting grim-faced beside me, a real panic overwhelmed me, as I started to wonder where I`d end up. "Where on earth are you taking me?" I asked feebly.

"Not that it matters, but it's the main-office in Stirling. We`ll be at the Station in perhaps half an hour, so you`d best just sit there and wait."

Trees, hedges, fields, hills, and houses all drifted by in a haze of bewilderment. None of it registered and not any of my predicament made an ounce of sense.

"Come this way." I was instructed, as I was briskly led to the back door of the Police Station, where I was ordered to take my shoes, and belt off, and to hand over money, phone, watch, coat, and rucksack; my persona stripped away. "Right; name, address, age, occupation, please." A Constable behind the desk demanded.

After this cheerless formality, I was led to the cells and locked up, the door slamming me in, and shutting out the rest of my life, it seemed.

Perhaps half an hour later, the door opened, and the same WPC informed me that I'd be here for the night, as my interview would need to wait until the necessary Officers came back on duty in the morning.

Aching all over, with dried blood on the various laceration, and several that I hoped were just severe bruises, I decided to assert my rights. "Look, it's pretty obvious I've been badly injured, and whatever mistakes may have been made in my arrest, I demand to get medical attention, now, please."

"I can't comment on your arrest Mr Borthwick, but I will see what can be done for you and your wounds. I think there may be a doctor at the station on another matter;" at which, the door slammed once more.

More time, more despair, continuing pain. I waited.

Eventually, a lady in smart clothes and not in a Police Scotland uniform entered.

"I've been asked to have a look at you, eh, Mr Borthwick. Dearie me, what on earth has happened to you?"

The doctor's arrival raised my spirits ever so slightly, as I did feel that in one respect, my needs were perhaps going to be addressed. "I was violently assaulted by a stranger up there in the hills, and thrown over a crag."

"I see;" she intervened. "Oh, I'm Doctor Springer. Well, it will be for the Police to determine what may or may not have happened. Let's look you over though." After ten minutes of poking, prodding, and questioning, she pronounced that there seemed to be no fractures. She turned her attention to lacerations on the head, arms, and knees. "I'll clean these up a bit; then it won't look quite as bad." That done she said; "I think we've met before, but for the life of me, I can't think where or when. What did you say you do for a living?"

"Social Worker with young offenders, or was until a few weeks back, as I jacked it all in."

"Were you at some conference or meeting over at the University about a year ago, perhaps? Something to do with youth offending? Must have been there because of my occasional link with Cornton Vale Prison."

"Yes, I was indeed;" some positive link to clutch at now crept into our conversation.

"Hm, seems you may be on the other end of things right now, but sorry, can't talk about that."

In desperation, I asked; "could you do one thing for me, in addition to the attention you've given to my injuries, that is, and for which I'm very grateful to you."

"Shouldn't really, but what did you have in mind? You'll need to be quick."

"They've taken my phone. Could you call my partner Liz and just tell her I'm OK?"

"As I said, shouldn't really". But the Doctor then gave me her notebook to write the name and number down. "OK, will see what I can do. It's an Edinburgh number." But her question was cut short, as the WPC re-entered.

"Everything OK, Dr Springer?"

"Yes, I'll be on my way now;" she winked back at me as she went out of the door, which once again slammed.

145

Oh fuck, Liz will be wondering where her car is, I thought in panic, as I slumped back on the hard, uncomfortable bunk.

Visiting young offenders in the cells had been one thing, but being incarcerated myself was quite another. If I`d thought about it at all, I might have recognised an affinity with their fear, despair, and even rage, but I was far too preoccupied with my predicament. Something masquerading as an evening meal was presented, and although hunger and the need for food were far from my thoughts, I did try to eat a little of it. It would be a long night. And so, it was, tedious, heart-searching, anxious, and all quite unresolved.

Whether it was sleep or just the effects of utter exhaustion, I must have drifted into something less conscious, which was shattered crudely, as yet-another Police Officer banged on the door and entered briskly. The constable was carrying a tray with a mug of tea and some toast on it. "Eat up, because you are due to be interviewed shortly;" with that, he was gone from the cell. I was surprisingly, glad of the offering, even if half the bones in my body still ached.

"Come this way Mr Borthwick;" as a man in a smart suit signalled for me to follow him to a room that had Interview Room 1 marked on the door. "Sit down, please. My colleague is just coming. Don`t imagine the cell was too comfortable."

Too true, was the first thought that came to mind. "What am I being interviewed for, what am I supposed to have done?" I pleaded.

"All in good-time;" as another man in a dark blue suit, collar, tie, and shiny shoes, entered.

Confirming my details all over again, I agreed that they were correct.

"Now, what were you doing up there in the hills yesterday, and why were you there?"

"Walking, camping, and exploring the area."

"Why?"

"Eh, because I wanted to. Nothing more sinister than that."

"I see. Well, it has been alleged, that about mid-afternoon yesterday, someone answering your description assaulted a man, and attempted to, eh, push him over the cliff."

"You do look like you have been in a fight. How do you explain that?"

"It was me that was beaten up, and then thrown over the cliff. Luckily, I got stuck on a ledge not too far down. Otherwise, you`d be interviewing a corpse."

"Less of the smart stuff Mr Borthwick. I see that your car, which is not registered to you as owner, was parked in the car park at the reservoir. Where did you go from there?"

"Up the hill, past some wind turbines, and to the cairn at the top of the hill. I camped up near the cairn."

"Are you in the habit of camping at the top of hills?"

"Yes, I am, I walk, climb and camp a lot. Top of a hill is as good a place as any if the weather is OK."

"And was that just one night of camping?"

"Yes, it was."

"Oh, I see a report of a car, must be your car, being parked overnight. Someone from Scottish Water made the report. Yes, but it's not your car. Do you know who the registered owner is, and do you have permission to use it?"

"It's my partner Liz Fergusson, 17 Lauderdale Street, Edinburgh, who owns it. And yes, I have her permission. Of course, I do. And what's more, I'm insured to drive it too."

This questioning was getting to me, as it didn't seem to be taking us any nearer to who my assailant had been, and how he'd set me up. Keep cool.

"So, you describe Liz, eh, Miss Fergusson as your partner, and she lives in Edinburgh, whereas you say you live in Peebles. Odd?"

"Not odd at all, that's just the way we like it."

The second blue suit tapped his colleague on the shoulder, and I could just hear part of what he said, but it included the words `at the desk`.

"OK, we'll leave your domestic arrangements at that Mr Borthwick."

"Did you see anyone else, when you were on the hill and camping?"

"Only a small group of two or three that came to look at the wind turbines just after me, and a couple possibly on the other hill across the wee valley yesterday evening."

"You say possibly? How many?"

"Two, I reckon, certainly more than one."

"Are you certain that you saw no one else?"

"Yes, because I like to note how much I've got the place to myself. Just one of my harmless obsessions. Oh, now that I remember, I did meet two youngish guys on a quad bike, shooting hares to reduce the ticks, they said."

"Have you had any other recent contact with the Police?"

"Yes, as it happens, I have, I've been brutally assaulted on several occasions. But I can assure you that it is me that has been on the receiving end. And since I'm completely unaware of who my assailant is, was, and as far as I'm aware, your colleagues elsewhere have been unable to identify him either, I'm anxious about the whole situation. Pretty certain you'll have all this on file."

"Yes, we do. But on the face of it, yesterday was different, as it was you who was reported as having done the assaulting. Looks odd."

"It's odd as two different socks, all right, but I can assure you that I've been set-up. Why, for God's sake if I had done the assaulting, would I have wrecked Liz's car beforehand?"

"OK, wait here, my colleague and I need to discuss this."

Left on my own, my heart pumping with rage, I wanted one thing only, and that was to get out of this place and regain my freedom.

They returned, having left their notepads elsewhere. "Right, Mr Borthwick, you are free to go. You would appear to have been set-up, as you put it. We will continue our investigations. There's a young lady waiting for you at the desk."

Chapter Seventeen

Just three days later, and emerging from my tent in Rhidorroch once more, after a reasonably good night, despite some lingering aches, I packed a few things needed for a day re-visiting this strange and beautiful place. Having plotted the watershed to the north and west of where I'd camped, I decided to follow this meandering ribbon in the landscape.

As I rounded the crag that overlooked the rock-rimmed lochan, I could see that to the north, a cloud inversion created a mysterious landscape, or perhaps it should be a seascape, as only tops the higher of the hills projected through the white spread of cloud that I was looking down on. And this mass of white seemed to be flowing slowly, pouring over some of the ridges and filling the hollows which merged with the surrounding white and somehow emptied just as quickly. Away to the north-west, I could see many of the much bigger mountains stand out like islands in this unreal sea. I became completely absorbed in identifying some of the distinctive shapes; Stac Pollaidh, Quinag, and further east from these the quartz topped watershed summit of Conival and her neighbour, Ben More Assynt. I felt truly connected with the great forces of nature and the wildness she had bestowed. Having read up all I could in this area, and learned of its geological significance, where tectonic plates had collided and then pushed younger rocks over the top of the much older ones, that had come in from elsewhere. It pleased me somehow that I was looking at the very landscape where some aspects of world geology had been discovered and interpreted.

Above, the sun was lifting higher in the sky, illuminating the white sea ebbing, and flowing at my feet. The violence that had been inflicted on me so recently seemed to be eclipsed by my present experience. This location was the greatest tonic, the finest uplift imaginable.

With each turn in my route around the countless often un-named lochans, and cresting the tops of hills with glorious almost unpronounceable names, a new vista would open in front of me. The white sea of the cloud inversion had ebbed into nowhere, and more distant island prospects off the west coast drew eye and spirit beyond the present shores. While inland, great clutches of mountains described a restless horizon.

My destination today, however, was here in the heart of Rhidorroch, and a mossy area fringed by rocky crags and lochans. It was here that I had met The Spirit who had entrusted in me with the quest for the Seven Signs. My purpose today, was to meet up with him once more, if at-all possible. After a few miles of stravaiging across the rough and wild, I found myself looking down on the special mossy area. I sat down on a rock to survey the scene, and to have a brew up. Nature can only be truly, fully experienced in gentle silence and contemplation, so I was quickly caught up in that spirit of openness, where time has no bearing.

My consciousness brought me slowly out of that state, and I realised that the ancient figure of The Spirit had appeared down here among the moss domes; he somehow drew me towards himself.

I was immediately struck by how frail he now looked. His familiar attire hung looser on him, and his shoulders were even less pronounced than they had been just a few weeks earlier.

"Hello, dear friend;" I said rather cautiously because I found that I was indeed nervous because of the way I found him to be.

He signalled me to sit down beside him on a rock at the edge of the mossy area and said: "I am tired, very tired, but I do want to know how you have fared in discovering and interpreting the Seven Signs. What you have made of tracing all that they together represent in our precious landscapes?" He paused, obviously waiting for me to respond.

"I am so glad to meet you again there's much to report."

This news seemed to perk him up and lifted him a bit.

"I've worked out the basic meaning of each of the Seven Signs, and then from that, I've plotted a line on the map that demonstrates exactly what it is. It is the watershed of Scotland. It may be geographic, but it has a much more profound significance bound up in the Seven Signs. I'm certain that what I have found is indeed what you entrusted to me; what I feel you somehow called me to do. It's a huge responsibility but is one that I'm honoured to take forward, and share more widely. A friend who's a researcher and environmental journalist is helping me with this quest." At this point, I could see his shoulders rise, and his form become more positive; it was like a burden had been lifted.

"There is, however, something that I must tell you, and it is this; someone or some organisation doesn't like what I'm doing. They are determined to sabotage my efforts. There have now been three attempts to kill me. I think it's the same person who has tried on each occasion, but he is very elusive, and I very much fear that he may strike again. The only suspicion that I can see about his motivation is that he somehow represents entrenched and traditional landowning interests; yes, an entrenched environmental mindset."

I could see that The Spirit was troubled by this news.

"I am indeed sorry that this quest has involved so much danger for you. It should have been an entirely enjoyable and fulfilling gentle experience, as it has so much to offer. I believe it to be the finest single discovery for the people of Scotland who love the wilder land and are uplifted by the spirit of wildness. That it should be opposed so fervently is strange and troubling."

"Yes, I can see that you will be saddened by this, but I vowed to take on the quest, and you've my assurance that I'll not be deflected from it. You've my word on that, and I'll be ever more vigilant. If I'm correct about the old, or secretive landowning interests, then it may just be that they see it as a threat in the context of the contemporary land reform era that we are going through right now. Land reform is popular and currently very necessary in Scotland, so that is what will prevail, and whatever opposes it will be side-lined; utterly. Your Seven signs will triumph; I will make sure of that."

Our parting was in the silence of a deep affinity.

My emotions were all over the place as I walked those couple of miles back to the tent. Weaving round lochans and outcrops, negotiating my way through areas thigh-high with moss domes or tussocks, and with great boulders seeming to lour over me. Only the landscape's cold spectrum of black and grey touched me.

The tent had taken a fair battering overnight, as the weather had changed quite suddenly at around dusk the previous evening, so waking to a wild start to the day, it was clear that I'd be carrying some wet gear back out from Rhidorroch. I lay for a while listening to the wind and rain and looked at the light alloy tent poles bending and flexing under strain. The fabric of the tent moved with the poles, with the inner and outer often getting very close together; this was a familiar experience. Somehow, though, that didn't happen, as the design and tensions could adjust; just in time. Streams of water ran down the outer, rolled into bigger flows, and were lost immediately in the vegetation around the tent. Although the weather appeared by sight and sound to be in the tent with me, I knew from experience that I was safe and dry within my light fabric shell.

Lying there, I thought on the previous day's venture to find The Spirit, and on how long that quest had taken. I thought too, on how frail he looked, but took comfort in the fact that he had looked at peace with the world and himself, when I had reported on all that I'd done, and intended to do. Although troubled by the dangers encountered, and the apparent opposition both to my, or should I say, our quest, he seemed content with what I might do with it. But he was resolute in his conviction that it was right, and that my course of action was the correct one. I could see in his ancient eyes that he was bestowing his blessing, a benediction on it all, and knew for certain that Scotland and her people would gain so much from it. Although I could never have acknowledged such things, a few weeks earlier, he conveyed without words being necessary, a conviction of the potential benefits for the human spirit, and as he gestured around us, he was clearly implying the spiritual experience we could gain from our closer gentler interaction with the Natural world.

I would not be saddened in any way if this was The Spirit's final gesture because he knew his task, his purpose was almost complete, and that he had entrusted it wisely. I was of course immensely humbled by this trust placed in me, despite the dangers I'd faced. In an odd way, I took the forces that seemed to be pitted against me, as a compliment, for them, or it represented one of the final vestiges of something that was now almost played out, and indeed, it soon would be consigned to history, where it belonged. For surely, I told myself, when something so intrinsically positive meets such a response, the good in it is tempered in the fire and becomes so much the stronger for it.

This storm without raged some more, but my mind and soul were on a real high. I could feel the true spirit of place welling up within me, and a profound peace was transporting my spirit to somewhere it had never been before. Here, here on the lands above the waterheads, was something unique, generous, and almost beyond measure. The tears were flowing gently down my cheeks, as I drifted off to sleep once more. Was this a right-of-passage into the spirituality of Nature`s riches?

Waking once more, I became conscious of the calm outside the tent. The tempest had ceased, and a radiant light seemed to fill the area around. Looking out of the small window, I could see that all-of Rhidorroch that was within sight was bathed in it too. It was real, and not in any way imagined.

Time to make a move then, so I started to pack some of my gear, and to emerge from my sleeping bag to get fully dressed. Opening the flaps of the tent, and on crawling out, I put my boots on. Breakfast and tea followed, and I felt that perfection that comes with contentment. Even if I had more trials in my quest to endure, I would do so with the knowledge that the simple goodness in it would prevail; it would triumph.

Chapter Eighteen

The mug of coffee Liz was holding was still steaming, as I came into the bar of the hotel to greet her. She rose as I walked forward, we embraced; exchanging our usual warm eager greetings when we'd been apart for a few days.

"Been waiting long, when did your train get in?" I asked warmly.

"Och, about half an hour, and it took me a wee while to walk down from the station, so this coffee and some shortbread, which I've eaten were welcome. Didn't fancy the culinary offerings from the trolley on the train. I'd a meeting in Glasgow first thing, about bringing some students to one of the Galleries in the Autumn, but managed to get away pronto to catch this train to Bridge of Orchy, at the back of twelve. Hey, it's so good to see you Pandy. What sort of a journey have you had, hope my car was behaving itself? Oh, and I haven't checked us in yet," gesturing to her rucksack and overnight bag.

"That's OK, can I get a coffee and shortbread first too, though, as I've not stopped at all on the journey down?"

"Of course, I'll get it for you, my love."

Watching her walk over to the bar to order, I was as ever, struck by all that so appealed to me about this lady; passion, poise, and purpose.

"Took me just over the three hours, most of the road was good and not too busy. Managed to meet up with my friend Colin in Ullapool for a coffee before I set off, which was great. His local knowledge, especially of the mountains all around there is pretty impressive."

As the coffees arrived, it occurred to me that I was hungry, and asked: "Have you had any lunch?"

"No, thought I`d wait for you, but the soup will be fine for now."

Before the waiter left, I ordered two bowls of soup to keep us going.

After all my mishaps and dangers on previous outings, Liz was keen to know that this one to Rhidorroch had been safe and that at the very least, I was none the worse for it.

"Yes, it was fine indeed, the weather was a bit mixed, as usual, but that's not a problem, and I did eventually find The Spirit. Very sad in a way, as he looked so frail. Was left with a feeling that he knew his journey`s almost over; can only describe his appearance as showing a kind of spiritual peace, though. Hope that doesn`t sound daft, what little he did say to me carried the conviction for him that he`d entrusted the Seven Signs with the right person, in me."

"Dear God Pandy, that sounds like a big responsibility that you carry for somebody that you clearly care about."

"Yes, it is, and I do, but it`s not a burden in any way. The more I`m involved, and the more that something seems determined to scupper the quest, the deeper my resolve to see it through to completion and success, whatever form that might take."

"You are some man, my dearest Pandy, but I`m worried that what seems stacked against you might just win through, then where would we be?" Liz said, her voice faltering.

Pushing the empty dishes aside, I put my hand gently on hers, and said: "Yes, I do know you are worried, and it`s probably unfair of me to inflict this anxiety on you. You have my word, that I'm now especially vigilant, will look out for myself, and therefore for us, my love. Listen, let's continue this later. Promise I'm not ducking it, but let's get checked-in and sort our gear for the next few day's climbing before we get dinner."

"Ae` that's good, and I'll hold you to it."

"Sound. The stuff in the car is a bit of clutter, so it'll take a couple of journeys to bring it all in. Tent probably needs drying. But will leave my boots in the car."

We made our way to the reception, and the same waiter who'd served us soup appeared in his new role, checking us in, and giving directions to the room, as he handed me the key.

"Sorry it's a twin, but we are pretty busy, and that's what was earmarked for you by my colleague." He said as he referred to the computer screen.

"That's OK;" Liz said. "We'll be fine."

The stairs creaked, as we made our way up to what must have been an older part of the building, and entered a large north facing room. Twin beds, sure enough.

"Take your pick, Liz. Near the door or the window, your choice? I'll go and get some more of my stuff from the car."

"Think I'll go for the window, Andy. It's also nearer the radiator."

"And there was me thinking I could devise a way to provide the personal warmth for you, somehow;" I said in a slightly scoffing manner.

"You'd need to re-organise the room."

"Greater things have been achieved; many's time. Back soon."

The contents of the car weren't just as disorganised as I'd feared, so could get my rucksack on my back and a large holdall in my left hand.

The bedroom furniture was duly re-arranged, and following a slow dinner in the lounge bar, during which, there was much to be discussed. Later, we proved the effectiveness of the new layout of our billet.

A thick blanket of mist reduced visibility to no more than fifty yards, as we drove a couple of miles along the road to Auch for the start of our three-day venture. Parking beside another car near the farm, and leaving a route note on the passenger seat, we hoisted our rucksacks onto our willing backs. Walking south along the West Highland Way, we discussed some of the detail of what we'd agreed the evening before. Liz was very amenable to my suggestion of following the watershed route in this area; we'd exploit the opportunity, should it arise, for her to get some photographs. The mist threatened to put paid to that aspiration, but in an ever-positive mood, she reminded me of the possibilities of a close-up of droplets of water on a spider's web, or on the early grasses. No opportunity was to be missed, and if it meant me hanging around while she set up a shot, I assured her that I'd be glad to help her creative effort. We were in no great hurry.

"When we get to the watershed, we'll find we've a brutal six hundred metres of ascent, but that'll get us up out of the valley, and onto the hills."

A Highland cow looked at us quizzically through the bars of a high gate, as we walked along chatting, towards the start of the big climb; if only it could know the care that had gone into packing these rucksacks. Although we'd done it so often before and should have been an expert, we'd acknowledged that no two outings were ever quite the same. Without saying anything to this effect, we knew that Liz was slighter in build than me. She always insisted however in carrying her share. Clothing, equipment, and food were distributed between our rucksacks accordingly; both of us were happy with the arrangement.

On reaching the line of the fence that disappeared off up into the mist to the left, on that rapid ascent that we must follow, we paused however for a snack bar each; "to give us an energy boost" as Liz said, to add to her spirit of determination. No conversation between us was possible for the next hour or so, though, as we scrambled and puffed our way up the unstable scree. But as the line of the fence then eventually started to curve out over such horizon as there was, we suddenly found ourselves and the hill in the clear bright sunshine.

Still speechless, but with pleasure, we simultaneously slowed our pace to take in the splendour and riches of the new world that we'd entered upon, it was one of those magical moments that climbing is occasionally blessed with. Walking, almost dancing, on the short grass, with firm footing, we were soon at the cairn marking the summit of the first hill. Without the need to consult, we sat down side by side on the sunny side of the pile of stones and were instantly at one in the vast clear views that surrounded us. The three-sixty-triumph, as I liked to call it.

Throughout the day, we walked on tops and ridges cresting the higher ground that is the watershed. With camera in hand, much of the time, Liz was captivated by the colours, textures, and shapes of lichen on the rock, she would pause to record how she saw the light as it illuminated stems of the burgeoning moor grasses or tender mosses in some sheltered hollows. A lochan provided exceptional reflections of the neighbouring hills and cloud wisps. I was happy to watch how she positioned herself for each shot, and looking this way and that, for the place of the sun. On one occasion, we waited for over an hour for something to be just right, captured the moment, and moved on; enjoyment in what she was doing, was intense.

When I wasn`t watching Liz, it was the distant views and the horizon that held my attention. There was an almost endless array of mountains calling out to be identified and named, and I went to some lengths to trace the likely route of the watershed amongst all these possibilities. The day was filled busily with avid attention to detail and distant prospects, in equal measure.

Descending cautiously to a bealach in the early evening, we set about finding a good pitch for the night. With an ancient stalkers track running through the glen, there were several close-grazed firm areas to choose from, but we opted for one right on the watershed, that had a burn descending towards it before turning sharply to mark which way it would drain. If this was a pilgrimage, we were truly on the holy ground.

Having been confined to our thoughts and interests, for most of the day, but the one complimenting the other, the silences were overtaking by more conversation, once our shelter for the night and dinner had been dealt with.

"You`ll have quite a bit to upload, when you get home, as I can`t imagine how many photographs you`ve taken; you were away in a world of your own." We sat drinking our tea, as the light was beginning to fade.

"Don`t think I was counting Pandy, though I guess I could consult the camera. You`re right, though; I was captivated and getting quite carried away. When the circumstances are right, I just allow myself to be focussed completely on capturing whatever takes my fancy. With you here to navigate, I`d not to give that need a second thought, but this kind of experience has happened before when we`ve been out together. Perhaps what`s special about this is that we weren't in any hurry, and didn't need to get to the top of the mountain. The conditions were good too, perhaps a bit sunny in the middle of the day, but ach, just a chance to indulge myself. I hope you'd a good day trailing along behind me or steering me from the aft."

"This watershed gives a chance to look at the mountains in an entirely new way, looking at what connects them way beyond their immediate groupings. I've had a whale of a day. If I'd been so inclined, I could have picked out and named all the mountains I've, we've, climbed in this part of Scotland, it was so incredibly clear. Reckon I could see peaks thirty or forty miles away. Although that cloud inversion earlier on gave a weird island sensation, when it cleared, the connections became even fuller, and more complex, and I could make much more sense of the detailed panorama. I was in a trance, some of the time, for sure."

"Glad you got what you wanted out of it."

"One of the intriguing things was the overall lie of the land. Since we are on the kind of spine of the country, no matter how much it meanders this way and that, we know that one side is bound for the North Sea, and the other for the Atlantic. Someone I was talking to recently said something to the effect that this must divide Scotland, but I much preferred to see it as something that brings the whole country together, from the English border all the way to the far northeast and everything in between, including Cumbernauld, of course. Can't think of anything else which achieves that sense of environmental connectedness; the scale of it is almost mind-blowing. And connected by what, I hear you ask? By nothing more profound than wildness; that too is utterly mind boggling."

Refilling our mugs, we revelled in the time we were having together, sharing a common experience but each in our distinctive ways.

The night must have continued the calm of the day, for we slept well; with the music of the burn from nearby, as an entirely natural gentle sound system.

Next day began much the same as the previous, with dense mist enclosing our little camping world, but a breeze had added something new to it while we'd slept. Busying ourselves with all the business of breakfast, ablutions, and packing up, we realised that the outside of the tent was carrying a sheet of moisture. So, by shaking as much of this off as possible, it had to be packed wet, and just hoped that we'd get the right conditions to dry it out during the day.

Another steep ascent started the day, with a bit of care being needed to pick a route avoiding crag and loose scree, wherever possible. As we climbed, so the wind increased.

Although the route for the day was a similar mix of tops and ridges, it was marked out by that familiar combination of blustery wind, squally showers, passing periods of mist which meant we'd to navigate with care. Then came the welcome spells of bright clear sunshine, when the views would suddenly open to give tantalising wide vistas, and just as quickly be snatched away by the all-enveloping clag once more. The conversation between us was infrequent, but in a strange way, I could see that we were both invigorated by the variety, the occasional challenge, and the hope that another window on the world would open for us.

By lunchtime, there was less of the rain, and mist, so we stopped near a hill-top and sat in the lee of a cairn. Taking a quick chance to get the tent dried out, it was spread on the ground and anchored to big rocks, where the wind caught at it as it billowed and flapped frantically; it dried within half an hour, while we had our lunch.

By evening we'd reached another bealach, which carried a track over to Loch Lyon, but turning west, the descent was rapid, where a more sheltered spot was readily found for the night. Following the well-rehearsed routine of camping, cooking, eating and getting water for the next day we turned in, as the dusk was falling around us.

"Remember that conversation we had a wee while back about dark secrets, Andy?"

"Sure thing, I'll not forget that in a hurry, had started recalling a difficult episode in my life from years ago, when I nearly got beaten up by you for my troubles. But don't worry, I forgive you. Why?"

"Well, there's been something bugging me, that I feel I should be telling. Perhaps it's all this danger you've been in lately, that makes me want to be sure that we are OK, and well, completely open with each other. At one, if you like."

"That's a bit ominous, but yes, do go on;" I said rather doubtfully, and wondering what on earth was coming.

Liz took a deep breath as if to brace herself for some confession, or big revelation. "Remember when we started going out together Andy?"

"Yes, I do. It was pretty special, at least I thought so at the time, and I'm very pleased with the way it's all worked out since."

"Well, there's one thing I wasn't honest with you about at the time. Guess I was just a bit economical with the truth, as I really didn't set out to be in any way dishonest."

"Go on."

"We'd first met at that gathering about something environmental, or perhaps it was political, I think. Might have been about community buy-outs or something. Anyway, then we met up again at someone's party the following weekend."

"Yes, I do remember that, and I thought to myself, she's lovely, a grand sense of humour, and quite a smart body too; this must be fate. But what's this to do with you unburdening your soul?"

"Scene setting, perhaps, as I felt pretty much the same about you. Anyway, you asked me out, and although I was a bit hesitant at first, you were persuasive, and wouldn't take no from me."

"Do you blame me, I was keen."

"No, not then or now, but things weren't quite as simple as I may have given the impression. The reason I was hesitant, as you put it, is that I was engaged at the time. Oh, dear God, now I've told you."

I could hear her sobbing lightly, even against the sound of the breeze puffing at the tent, and the occasional raindrop mixed in with it. It was hard to know how I should or could react to this news; it had come out of the blue.

"You'd better tell me more, as although this has come as a surprise, I've no doubt you want to get the whole story off your chest. So, go on and tell; please."

After a long pause, in which the wind and rain came and went in bursts, we lay there in our sleeping bags surrounded by night. Liz eventually said; "Thanks, Andy, I do need to tell, and just hope that you don't think any less of me at the end of it. Yes, I'd got engaged to a guy named Anthony, about eighteen months earlier, and we'd started thinking about our plans. But the more I thought about them, the more my doubts grew. Mummy had encouraged out friendship, relationship, and the more I thought about it, the more trapped I felt, between all that, and what I wanted for myself. Didn't want to hurt Anthony, as he was a nice, if ineffectual guy; a harmless wimp, as I now see it. There was nothing about him that excited me. The family connection is that he went to the same prep school as Jamie. God help us, it may well have been Jamie that introduced us."

"Bugger me, that's not a good start." I gasped.

"True, and that as well. Anyway, along you came when I was caught right in the middle of wondering what to do."

"Sounds a bit like you used me then, Liz. But maybe that's getting ahead of things. Go on."

"No, I did not use you Andy, or at least I definitely did not set out to do that, not at all. And you've just said that to start with I was a bit cautious, or hesitant. So now you know why. Not without principle, you know."

"Yes, I know that Liz."

"Well I was persuaded by your determination, or whatever it was, so we went out together a few times, and one thing led to another, as it does, or so I discovered. Then we went off on that climbing weekend in May to Kintail. You, romantic swine that you are, treated us to a couple of nights in the Cluanie, and I discovered, well you know what I discovered, and that clinched it for me."

"Oh, oh, still using me a bit here, to solve a problem in another part of your life, or in your head, at least."

"Andy, I never set out for it to be this way, honest, that's why I've never said anything about it before. The longer I didn't say anything or tell you, the harder, the more impossible it got. Please trust me. This is so very hard for me."

Her sobs sounded very genuine and heartfelt.

Once she'd composed herself, Liz continued; "I could go on at length at what a great guy you were that weekend, and indeed you still are. I'd never had anyone pour my bath for me before, other than my mother perhaps. There was something so thoughtful, considerate, about you. Mind you; I was a bit surprised when you then jumped into the bath beside me."

"Don't think that's got much to do with this confession of yours Liz."

"Perhaps not, but I discovered that you had character, you could be very caring, and you'd a good bit of spark about you. But when we got back home, I met Anthony the very next evening, and broke it to him, that our engagement and relationship was over. Put it as kindly as I possibly could, but he went to pieces. I'd made my mind up, and stuck to it. Over the next few weeks he tried everything to get me to change my mind; phone calls, flowers, cards, the lot. Thankfully, I was staying in my flat, so my family, Mummy, knew nothing of this. I just hoped she wouldn't find out some other way. She didn't I'm glad to say, as I knew I'd to tell her myself. A few weeks later, I plucked up the courage. I do love her, but there's a cold respectability about her, that's rather daunting or unfeeling."

"We met up in The Roxburgh, for a chat, as I put it. When I told her, she was speechless at first, but soon launched into a focussed, but controlled rant. Anyway, I managed to hold my ground. We parted with a gulf between us; I'd never encountered before. I imagined she'd be wondering how she was going to explain this to her pals. I decided that was her problem."

"Then she phoned me that evening and put it straight to me, asking if there was anyone else. I just said that one failed engagement was quite enough for now, and had to hang up. My turn to go to pieces. But if I was a bit distracted around that time Andy, now you know why."

"Well, you did seem a bit strange, looking back on it now, but I just concluded that all new relationships can go through a bumpy patch, but didn`t take it too personally; how could I?"

"There you have it, Andy; I wasn't entirely honest with you, I`m not proud of myself, and am very sorry."

"Only criticism I`d have, is that you didn`t tell me sooner. It's a damned shame that you've carried this around with you all these years Liz. Think I can see why you did what you did, or didn`t. Guess you`d no more idea than me, how things would have worked out between us. They`ve worked out well, or at least I think so. And that's despite the testing it's had over the past few weeks. Rest easy my love, because telling me will have made you feel a whole lot better, and I`m absolutely fine with it."

Chapter Nineteen

Our parting in the morning came easily for us. We'd spent a rewarding time together on the hill and in our tent, and our understanding of each other had found new depth. Now, Liz had business to attend to back in Edinburgh, and I'd a mountain meander planned for a'Cruach on the north side of the vast wildnesses of Rannoch Moor. Making good-time on the walk out, despite a change in the weather, we reunited Liz with her car, and after a fond embrace, I set off to the north on the West Highland Way. Although I was no great fan of such popular long-distance routes, their purpose and appeal were of value to many. It would serve my purposes too for the next few hours.

With the King's House Hotel and the Moor finally behind me, my meander resumed under what had been magically transformed into a clear dome of light blue. Stopping for a much-needed brew-up beside a moss-fringed lochan on the Rannoch Rim, I was transfixed by the bobbing heads of the early bog cotton that at that moment seemed to happily signal so much of the round of seasons and their continuity. Given the nature of the quest, this gladdened my heart, for I also saw those mosses and sedges where moor and loch embraced so sustainably. Which one of the seven signs this accounted for, I couldn't quite recall, but as I sat there sipping my black tea, my mind strayed to the importance of these living landscapes. It was very reassuring to think that were I to return here in perhaps a hundred years; these very plants could have turned into buried peat, and taken a load of carbon down with them. As a gesture of appreciation, I toasted the value of the long slow processes that I knew were taking place right here; all things about which The Spirit had been so eloquent about.

Ronald received another sequence of passion-laced eco reports from me during the many hours of exploration the following day. With a varied array of photos and the text to go with them, I was fulfilling my purpose in giving the fullest possible picture of the environmental delights of this area. But I went beyond the local, in order, to describe how it typified so much of the watershed meanderings through landscapes to south and north of here.

My choice of locations had been so carefully selected for their variety, terrain, elevation, and wider character, that I wanted it to build into a compelling visual and written argument. Drawing upon what a colleague had once described, as my love affair with wilder Scottish landscapes, I knew I was tapping into something rich and endlessly rewarding.

Strange, I thought, how the night time in a tent can be so full of great thoughts on the connectedness of all of Nature`s ways and wonders. Within the vastness of all the possibilities that I knew I was just beginning to embrace, suddenly I found myself contemplating the powerful notion of the watershed, as a being quite simply, the sleeping giant of Scottish landscape. My own insignificance against this most appealing of all images, was manifest so strongly in the present, as I realised that I was camped right on top of it.

That same inspiration carried me into the following day`s activity, my spirit soaring with the eagle keeping watch from on high.

A surge of panic ran through me as the sound of rifle shot came from somewhere behind echoing off crag and boulder. The first bullet missed, but I wasn't hanging around to see by how much. No sooner had I grabbed my rucksack than an agonising pain erupted in my left shoulder.

Oh fuck, this bastard means business, flashed through my mind, as I tried to assemble a scrap of a plan to save my life. Realising that the wound, while excruciatingly painful, wasn't at that stage life-threatening, giving myself a bit of hope that I could get away, somehow. Would be harder for him, assuming my assailant was male, to re-load and fire while on the move over this very rough terrain; perhaps I'd have a minor advantage.

But I'd no way of knowing how fit he might be, or of his skill and accuracy with a rifle. His motivation to destroy me may have had me baffled, but I didn't doubt his utter determination; he had a mission.

Realising that I needed some appreciation of the terrain, rather than just running in a blind panic, I glanced this way and that, to try and get the measure of it. These brief, desperate thoughts were halted abruptly, with yet another shot, and it seemed to hit the heather some way in front, but directly ahead, my head. Christ, this psychopath has no compromise in him and is hell bent on my demise, I screamed in my mind, by now, too out of breath to think straight. If I die here, in this remote spot, my body may never be rediscovered, ever. My destiny would be to return to nature, just as imagined The Spirit might have done. But I was raving; having these ghastly thoughts, in such a desperate situation.

Think straight, I determined. Finding that I was somehow running south, and dredging, clutched at my memory of the map, were there any features on it which could be of any help, and assist in the escape? Then I remembered a wide strip of forest running right along the lower slopes of this hillside, between this hill and the great expanse of Rannoch Moor. Forest means cover, and Land Rover tracks, if I were to turn left heading east, I'd be getting over towards the railway, and to Rannoch Station; a scrap of hope, perhaps.

No sooner had I formulated this sketch of a plan than I found myself tumbling over and over down the steepening hillside. A flash of heather flew past my eyes, and the dark shape of a peat hag almost engulfed me. Tumbling and rolling very unevenly, I found that my rucksack was turning me blindly to left and right in one lurching uneven arc after another.

My stop had been every bit as abrupt as the start of this inferno of terror fuelled movement. Staring in sharp close-up focus at the lichen and bird shit on a huge grey boulder, I glanced to my left only to be startlingly confronted by the bleached skull of a long dead sheep. Empty eye sockets seemed to leer hideously at me in my agony. It was my right shoulder that got the impact of this collision.

No time to nurse wounds or assess the damage, I was up on my feet and away off down the slope once more, in a panic-stricken effort to get away from the gun-toting madman who was in pursuit. Once more, I found myself sprawling in the heather, as the remains of a rusty barbed wire fence lying half concealed in the vegetation grabbed my ankle. More pain, more blood, and if I'd had time to think about it, a pair of trousers wrecked, into the bargain. I heard a yell coming from behind as I reckoned, hoped, my assailant had encountered some obstacle too, which would slow him a bit. Perhaps, oh, dear God, perhaps, it would wreck his rifle too.

As I ran on, the forest got closer, and the welcome prospect of some cover reached out forlornly. Another shot echoed off the side of the forest, and I feared, the bullet had hit the side of my rucksack. With no new pain to endure, though, I reckoned he'd missed me, but I discovered from this that he could reload while on the move; this fucker had arms training; I was up against a professional. My heart sank.

The outer branches of the dark green forest trees came right down to the ground, but I knew I must penetrate this spiky Sitka wall, so I just threw myself at it, hoping, just hoping that the interior would be less dense down at my level at least.

Sure enough, I found myself within the darkness of the canopy overhead. Coming out of the daylight into such gloom, took what seemed like an age to adjust to, but row upon regimented row of very solid tree trunks confronted me. As if this wasn't enough, the remains of lower branches seemed to clutch out, grab or threaten to skewer me; it presented a new threat. Having had to traverse this kind of forest before, I knew that I must find the way in which it had originally been planted. Frantically, I tried to work out the direction in which the lines of trees were growing and to find the slight ditch that would lie between these rows. A glimmer of luck this time, as I found that they led down the slope and slightly off to the left; the very direction I needed.

Behind me, I heard more crashing and loud oaths. My assailant may be in the forest, but running through this lot with a gun would be an added difficulty for him. Where possible, I skipped across a few lines of trees to be less visible. I realised, however, that these sharp protruding branches were systematically destroying my outer clothing, and while I sought to protect my face, it too suffered a few lacerations.

Hope once again surged through me, as I saw a band of lighter pine branches ahead, and reckoned that it would be evidence of either a forest ride or perhaps even a track. As I fell headlong down the steep cutting on the top-side of it, I met the mud and gravel in close-up, once more. So now I was covered in grime to add to my blood stains. But this had indeed given me hope, as I could see where I was running, and much of it on a reasonably even surface. It may have given me an equal chance, but the gunman at my rear, cancelled that out instantly, for as soon as he was on the track, another shot echoed along the avenue.

Taking off as fast as my legs could endure, I did however try and get into a pace that my lungs could cope with too, so in an odd way, I contented myself with a fast trot; unless he were Superman, he would fair no better. The track took several turns to left and right, crossed the occasional concrete bridge, and thankfully continued a gentle downhill trend. The blur of countless dark green trees drifted past without note. Knowing I was beginning to feel the pace, the pain, and the despair, I knew too, that I must somehow keep going, or I'd be history.

The sight of more light ahead signalled the edge of the forest and the more open moorland; change sometimes gives new impetus for survival.

Maintaining my pace as best, I could see that this was now in the open moor country, and therefore much more exposed. There was every reason to believe that this crazed lunatic behind me knew this as well, and would exploit it if the gun-totter could. I did hear him bellow out something like `come back here you bastard`. But there was little chance of that. The sight of Rannoch Station perhaps half a mile off, redoubled my effort and resolve. Perhaps it was clutching at a shred of hope, but I reckoned he was slightly less likely to shoot at me within or even near to this scattered settlement. The risk of witnesses perhaps.

The sight of a small white cottage to my right beside a loch, encouraged, but didn't divert me in any way. That could just as easily have been a trap. On hearing a train on the track, also to my right, and noting that it must be Fort William bound; I knew it would almost certainly stop at the station. Ahead of me, a high iron barred gate loomed, but I quickly reasoned that it might be locked, or tied with a tangle of wire, so getting over the top of it would be best. Launching myself into it, with every ounce of strength I could muster, another sharp crack from the rifle showed that nothing and nobody was safe from my crazed assailant. Although I did get over the gate, I landed badly, spraining my left hand, and sending another eruption of pain through that entire side of my body. The train was slowing as I got to it, and waited what seemed like an age for it to pass, so that I'd get around the back of it and onto the platform.

Utterly desperate, I could see the conductor slowly alight, look each away along the platform, assess who might be getting onto the train, and only then did he open all the doors. Oh fuck, this has given that bugger behind me an advantage, I gasped to myself. But I was on the train in one last desperate leap, the welcome door-closing sound echoed in my head, and then I saw my pursuer running along-side, frantically pressing the open buttons on every door, from the outside, as the train gathered speed. His gun was clearly visible to all the shocked passengers.

Chapter Twenty

Slumping onto one of the seats nearest to the door, I looked up and had very brief eye contact with my murderous assailant. His look said, `I'll get you yet`.

All I could catch of his appearance, as the train left him behind, was that he was dressed in camouflage clothing, as if on manoeuvres. His gamekeeper hat was out of kilter with the otherwise military appearance. Certainly, a bit older than me, he stood I guessed, about the same height or perhaps a wee bit more, and his weathered complexion was that of an outdoorsman. Something registered. And then he was gone.

At this point, I realised that everyone in the carriage was looking at me with visible horror. The ticket man approached in an obviously nervous manner, as I sat there gasping for breath, my rucksack still on my back, and both my clothing and what he could see of me covered in a mixture of blood, sweat, and mud.

"Jesus Christ, man, that was close. That madman seemed intent on killing you dead. But are you OK? Do you want me to stop the train and get help? Shall I call the Police, or better still perhaps, an ambulance?"

His questions had just about given me time to gather my thoughts, if not my breath. "Still alive, perhaps" I gasped. "Yes, that fucker was utterly determined to shoot me. In fact, one of his shots has hit me on the shoulder, or the top of my arm. I've been running from him for miles. Thank God your train came along just when it did."

The woman on the tea trolley appeared with a cup, which she thrust into my hands: "Here son, it's hot, sweet tea, that's the best we can do right now, get it into you."

Someone else appeared, and said, "I've some basic first aid skills." Looking at the ticket man, he then added; "do you have a first aid kit on board?"

"Yes, I'll get it, it's in the driver's cab. Also, need to let him know what's happening."

By now I was sweating profusely, but I forced myself to drink the tea. My breathing was easing a bit, and I was becoming more conscious of the various areas of pain and other aches, which were beginning to wrack my poor body. A kindly looking young man had sat down beside me, helped me to remove my rucksack and coat, and was gently wiping some of the mess off my face. He was handed some wipes by yet another passenger, and so tended my face more systematically, but with obvious care. They all seemed more intent on helping me, than finding out what lay behind the drama of this violent assault.

On his return, the ticket man handed the first aid box. "See what you can find in there, and use whatever you need. I'll go back to the driver and see what's the best course of action, but there's no advantage in stopping away out here in the middle of the moor. We are best to get you to somewhere that an Ambulance can meet you. I'd say you must get to a hospital, and the nearest's in Fort William. I'll hopefully end up speaking to the Police on the phone too. I'll say that you appear to have been shot at, that passengers are helping by doing what they can for you here, and that you are alive, breathing, but do need medical care. That OK pal?"

"Yes, that'll do, I'll probably survive here on the train to Fort William, but it's up to the Police and the paramedics. I'll be in their hands."

More hot, sweet tea appeared, limited attention was paid to some of my more visible wounds and lacerations, but there was agreement that the shoulder was best left alone for more expert help. Happy to receive this level of aid, I didn't want to get into the whys and wherefores of it all. The train rumbled on and stopped at a few more stations, which demanded the attention of the ticket man. But he returned, with the news that Police and ambulance would meet us at Spean Bridge. Meantime could I give him any brief information about my assailant, where he might have gone, and indeed where he'd first taken a shot at me. The Police may want to mount a helicopter-borne assault on the area.

In my quite confused state all I could think was that by now, my assailant would have evaporated into the heather on the moor. No chance of finding him by now.

At Spean Bridge station, the full uniformed reception party was there waiting, with blue lights flashing, and all the manpower ready to halt the traffic on the main road when the time was right. Paramedics boarded the train, and my state of injuries and mental capacity quickly assessed. A Police officer stood by, taking notes, but said that the questions would come later. Although clearly injured, and the extent of this was unknown, it was reckoned that I could at least walk slowly off the train, but would then be loaded onto a trolley of some kind on the platform.

Coming-too, in what I took to be the hospital, I was, I discovered now dressed in a hospital gown, had been patched up in some way, and was attached to a drip.

"Fuck me; this is for real".

My battered rucksack lay on the floor beside the bed.

First thing in the morning Morag appeared, having shown her determined streak by blagging her way in to see me; she was a welcome sight.

"Dear Lord, Morag, it's lovely to see you, but how did you know I'm here?"

Ah, there's a fine system of jungle drums hereabouts, so word just got around and came my way. Shootings of people are not that common an occurrence in these parts.

Listen, I've got to get to the Scottish Natural Heritage offices just north of Perth later this afternoon, for a meeting. How are you feeling, have they patched you up?"

Still a bit uncertain about just how patched up I was, I just said; "think I'm more or less OK. A few aches and pains to be sure."

"Do you want to get out of here, and get home, as I could give you a lift to Perth, and put you on the train there if that's any good."

This kind offer perked me up a bit, so I confirmed that it would indeed be good to get out and get home. "Guess we'll need to see what the medics say first, though.

"Sure, that's fine, I'll see if I can hurry them along a bit." So off she went and returned ten minutes later with the doctor that had tended me the night before.

My wounds and dressings were duly checked, along with blood pressure, vision, ability to comprehend some counting backwards, and a few other things. Finally, I was asked "Well, how do you feel Andy, and who's this very persuasive young lady?

"Och, I'm beginning to feel a good bit more with it now, thanks to the attention being given to me here, and had a reasonable night's sleep. And this is Morag, a good friend, who's been kind enough to keep an eye on me."

"Lucky man to have such friends. If you feel that you are OK to travel with her, then I'm happy to discharge you. You'll need to take it easy, and I'd urge you to visit your health centre clinic or doctor as soon as possible, once you get home. I see that you live in Peebles."

"Yes, and we've a good health centre, so I'll make an appointment as soon as poss. And thank you for all your care, and for agreeing to let me out."

"No bother, I suspect you're as strong as an ox, but being shot at isn't too good. Might I suggest you try and avoid such things in the future? There's a note here to get you to visit the Police station once you're out of here, so you'd better attend to that before you head down the road."

The visit to the Police was thankfully brief, as they just wanted to confirm some of the details from the statement that they'd taken from me the previous evening, though my recollection of that was a bit vague. They'd also taken a statement from the ticket man on the train, and had sent out a helicopter, but found nothing other than an empty rifle shell on the railway track at the Station. I gave them my now useless phone charger, with the bullet stuck in it.

"We'll get this off to ballistics, and see what they can make of it along with the rifle shell. It's all part of building the picture of who or what we might be up against. We've got all your details, so we'll pass a report on to your local Police, should anything else come up which needs attention. When we catch this, eh, person and any accomplices he might have, they're in deep, deep shit. But I didn't say that, of course."

"My God, I hope there's no need for any more Police or medics activity for me, I've had quite enough."

"I'm sure you have. Safe journey home now."

Liz answered the phone on the third ring. She was, she said delighted to hear from me, asked how I was, and when I'd be home from my travels or adventures. Little did she know! "It'll be about teatime, and I'll text you from Perth, as it'll be a lot clearer then which train I'll be on."

"OK, see you later, and I can't wait to see you my lovely Pandy."

Morag did most of the talking as we wended our rather indirect way to Perth, while I was propped up and made as comfortable as possible. I learned more about her job, her family, her aspirations, and so much more, but it all passed, just like the scenery, in a bit of a blur. Apologising for my lack of response to all this, she kindly reassured me that there was nothing to be worried about on that account, as she imagined the memory of being shot and then wildly pursued across Rannoch Moor by a heavily armed madman would be foremost in my mind. How right she was.

At Perth Station, she waited, and got me onto a train for Edinburgh, saw me settled, and was off, to the meeting for which she was already late.

`A kind and generous soul`, I mused.

Liz had even managed to persuade the ticket barrier man at Waverley Station to let her onto the platform to meet me off the train. Had she sensed that something was amiss, that yet another disaster had befallen me, I wondered cautiously?

As soon as we embraced, she felt me wince, and drawing back, looked me up and down, and inquired, "Well, what's happened this time Andy Borthwick. Nothing too serious I hope?

"Oh, a small matter of an encounter with a madman, and a night in the hospital, but I am OK," I stressed as confidently as I could.

"Oh, dear heavens, is there no end to this ghastly nightmare? You may be OK, this time. But someone has you as a marked man, don't they?"

"Yes, it appears that way, but I'm very nearly there with my quest, then together we can get ready for your great exhibition, as promised."

"Let's just get a taxi home to mine, and you can tell me all, in the peace and quiet."

"Thank you, my love, for coming to meet me. Believe me, I am most grateful, as I know how busy you are."

"You do come first in all of this Pandy, so my bits and pieces can wait another day or so."

Liz's flat in Lauderdale Street was warm and welcoming as ever, and the evening sun was flooding in through the west-facing windows; it all lifted my spirits. We spent the next couple of hours talking about my adventure as I called it. The questions flowed back and forwards, and the answers or comments echoed from this. My attempts at steering the discussion towards her forthcoming exhibition were futile; she was having none of it.

Although I said I wasn't very hungry, Liz insisted on making a quick, nourishing meal, which we ate slowly, and during which, the inquisition continued. Whether out of exhaustion or just the need to unburden myself, I decided to tell Liz a bit about my suspicions.

"We've been wondering and puzzling over who may be behind all of this, Liz. My suspicions are beginning to become a bit clearer, now. Given that the Police are so involved, they aren't going to let it rest until they've arrested the culprit, or culprits, now are they?"

"You mean there could be more than one? Christ, that is even more serious."

"Well yes and no. There is only one who has been my main assailant, and I got a brief glimpse at him, as the train drew away from Rannoch Station. I now realise that I'd almost certainly seen him before, in the company of someone well known to you, and you are going to have to brace yourself for this because it's going to be hard for you to take. Before I tell you, though, remember you are the most precious, dearest and by far the most appreciated person in my life."

"And you for me, by far, Pandy, but where is this leading?"

"It's leading to your brother-in-law, Jamie Ferguson. He's not the actual murderer, but he's in it up to his neck, alongside his accomplice."

There was a long silence, and Liz's face showed something of the dawning reality of all that this might mean. She looked in despair across the room to the mantelpiece and at the silver-framed picture of Hermione and the two girls; of her lovely nieces.

"What evidence do you have for this?" She asked curtly.

I outlined for her the sequence of chance events, the growing suspicions I was harbouring, and the weaknesses in it too. It was yet, far from conclusive. Oddly, one of the strongest clues was that apparently random remark of his after our lunch with Archie, that it may be too late. That remark has troubled me ever since, mithered away, and really got to me; too late for what, for fuck sake? Even before that, he`d told me to watch my back, at Charles`s wedding; that was no empty threat. That chance observation of him in the very odd company in Perth must have been part of it, and I now suspect that the person he was with, is the very same one as took those shots at me on Rannoch Moor, and tried to drown in a bog. It`s all beginning to add up, but a bit patchy for now. Jamie`s hand in it is pretty clear, though, albeit as a slightly lesser partner in crime."

The words were no sooner out of my mouth than Liz had the phone in her hand, had dialled, and handed it over to me.

"Just repeat to them, all that you have told me, Andy."

Her face was ashen.

Chapter Twenty-One

The road to the Divisional Police Headquarters in Eskbank, may be majestically lined by an avenue of mature beech trees, but there the sylvan experience ended for Jamie, as he was driven unceremoniously wedged firmly between two Officers; interrogation beckoned. With a few formalities at the front desk, where he surrendered much, he soon found himself being huckled upstairs and along grey corridors to a room marked `Interview 3`.

His erstwhile respectability in the community of Aberlady had been well and truly cancelled-out, as a Police Incident vehicle was parked unceremoniously on the communal grass outside his house, to proclaim his fall from grace. Neighbours were none too chuffed.

The interrogation, or interview as the Police preferred to call it, lasted much of the next two days, and while they did garner some information from Jamie, he managed to hold his ground on who his accomplice might be. After discussions with the consultant at the psychiatric unit in Perth, Jamie was released on bail, pending further enquiries, with the admonition that he shouldn`t go too far.

Returning to his house, by the same transport that had carried him three days earlier, he entered his house and instantly had a feeling that the whole place had been thoroughly rummaged. The Police left him with a note, that the dogs are in kennels, and doing fine.

Liz had heard nothing of this and pressed on with some post end of term tidying up at the University. She also focussed some time on plans for the new session, to get that out of the way, and to leave her time clear for the Liz Fergusson Exhibition: Impressions of Wildness.

In the forest behind Rannoch Castle, redundant stable buildings had a low stone cottage attached. Wood smoke from one of the chimneys hung around the courtyard, creating a settled blue haze. Within the sitting room of the cottage, the air was no clearer, and a hunched figure in rough tweeds, muttered to himself and gave the logs in the hearth an occasional kick. He was mulling over the apparent failure of the mission that he was set on, which had been sparked a while back by Mr Jamie. A few chance remarks by him on the need to frustrate the efforts of one Andy Borthwick, had sparked rather more than was perhaps intended.

`But why should I do things by halves`; he asked the dog at his feet? `My training was always to succeed at all costs, to defeat the enemy: act now and only consider any questions later`. The dismal prospect of no longer being up to the job hung over him. Just when he thought his purpose to thwart land reform, whatever that might be, had given his life real purpose, he found that he was up against a smarter foe. That bit of paper which Mr Jamie had given him which, listed places and dates had seemed like just a simple check-list. But the first four items lay without having been ticked; the last one must surely bring success. He looked forward to meeting Mr Jamie again shortly to report `mission accomplished`.

`Another dram to help me in my resolve`, he mused. `And surely the General will be pleased with my efforts, for I`m sure I heard him say something about, damned changes to the settled order of things, to one of his shooting guests. Yes, he`d surely like the

Andy Borthwicks of this world to be put in their place. I must bring success for the General, and for Mr Jamie`.

Looking round his smoke and fumes-filled sitting room, Jock felt comfortable with the well-used state of the furniture, the threadbare carpets, and the picture of Queen Victoria presiding over his mantelpiece. `Aye, hound, the settled order of things`.

The very name of the next, and final area, that I planned to visit and explore in my quest, conjured all sorts of fearful images in my mind, like something straight out of a Victorian drama; The Rough Bounds sounded like it would be the most extreme and wildest of all. Ronald and I sat in the corner of the Abbotsford Bar indulging ourselves in a combination of beer and fantasies about the romance of untamed landscapes; our imaginations soared. We`d moved on from the more factual dimensions to his research, combined with the elements of the story that I had fed-in to date. Since the whole quest had been borne out of mystery, and the improbable but none-the-less real figure of The Spirit now was the time we reckoned to give the imagination much more freedom.

Ronald was better equipped than I, to call-up the dreadful images that had been so popular within Romanticism, and the way that Nature and landscape were merged in that whole movement. As he spoke about the poets and painters and what they portrayed of the apparently grandest and most terrifying aspects of natural world, my mind raced ahead to what I might find or even experience in this area so grimly called the Rough Bounds. It wasn't fear which gripped me, but all the possibilities bound up in such a name as this. The words were nothing if not evocative both singly, and even more-so when brought together. Watching a bead of amber liquid slowly running down my glass, the word Rough, was the first, and I wondered what it might mean. The opposite of smooth certainly; not on the fairway; hungover; a bad experience perhaps; rugged; a first sketch or draft in the creative world; and so, my imagination ranged over all these, and many more possibilities.

Out of bounds, or even beyond the bounds; the bounds of belief; or reality; all took me to the limit and beyond; a romantic notion, without a doubt. Taking another mouthful of beer, I looked up to see Ronald studying me quizzically, as I'd clearly drifted off listening to his informed discourse on romanticism, and as he commented, into a world of my own.

"This is going to be quite a venture for me, Ronald. Although I've read up on the area and had some understanding of its character, it's going to be a very different kind of place. When you think of what has happened, or almost happened in the other places, it's quite a thought to be setting off there on my own, into the unknown even."

"Bloody hell Andy, you are allowing yourself more caution than we're accustomed to; this is Scotland, not outer Mongolia. But yes, this quest has turned out a lot more fraught with danger than you'd ever imagined possible, hasn't it. Thankfully the Police are on the case, does that reassure you?"

Only a bit I reckoned, only a bit.

"Och yes, you are right, my friend. I'll be sending you back some great images in words and pictures, and you can add that to everything else we've amassed about these lands above the waterheads. That's what matters, not my mental fantasies. Thank God this is indeed Scotland."

"Thankfully yes, Andy. That should reassure you I hope."

Pick you up about ten tomorrow morning. You've got all your gear at Liz`s? I need to confirm a couple of things before we go, with the folk I'm meeting on Skye."

"Ae` that's grand see you then," as we drained our glasses, left the bar, and stepped out into the evening air in Rose Street. A street famous for many things, not least of which were those ardent pub crawls of student days.

The journey north next day was mostly through drizzle and fog-inducing low cloud, but as we`d so much to talk about, our spirits were high.

"I came across a reference to an intriguing character, and author recently. I'll put together a few notes on him for you Andy, and he seems to capture something of the landscape and spirit thing."

Although he was around almost three hundred years ago, and was a minister of the Kirk, he seemed almost as interested in little people, fairies, and other spirits that inhabited the landscape than the spiritual well-being of his flock. His name was Kirk, Robert Kirk. But he`d have no qualms about writing convincingly about these things. Ahead of his times, a heretic, or just astute, he'll probably add a valuable historical dimension to all this. Probably something about him on Wiki, but I guess where you are going for the next few days will be pretty Wiki-less."

With a late lunch in Fort William, I stocked up on a few lightweight culinary luxuries to quell my appetite in the severe remoteness that lay ahead over the next few days. As I bid farewell to Ronald at Glenfinnan, it was with the knowledge that the remainder of the day would take me along paths towards my goal; into the Rough Bounds.

Camping in a good spot beside the river, and just far enough up the glen to be clear of the trees, all seemed set for a good night. But those lingering doubts and challenges to my resolve niggled. The fact that I'd told the Police about my suspicions regarding Jamie carried some reassurance, but my mind was not entirely at ease. The wounds I'd received on my last outing had not fully healed, and I knew I'd at least one more visit to make to the health centre to get it all checked out. Carrying a rucksack gave the occasional sharp shot of pain: but I was resolute. Once more, however, the knowledge that we were nearing the main conclusion of the quest, won through, and I drifted into a good place.

Overnight the weather cleared, and the new day had dried the outside of my tent. Busied myself with the morning routines of food, pondering over the route for today, packing up, and then getting on my way. With two mountain bealachs to cross to get to my destination for the day, at the western end of Loch Quoich, I put some mettle into my stride along tracks and paths that took me through the magnificent country, past the very occasional ruined cottage, and across burns that were easy to ford. My walking poles clicked on the ground in a rhythm which seemed to give emphasis to my purpose, and the gentle breeze kept the midges at bay.

Apart from being barked at by a collection of dogs in the stalker's kennels as I passed the scattered settlement of Strathan, only two other people came my way; a young couple who told me they were walking from Inverie on Knoydart through to Invergarry. They were celebrating the end of their exams together. "A very fine way to blow away the cobwebs;" I affirmed for them. "With much to celebrate, I'm sure."

Each bealach seemed to take me across from one world into yet another, as new enticing vistas opened-up ahead of me. Crossing the second of these, I could see on my map, that it was taking me over to the other side of the line I'd marked as the watershed. An auspicious moment perhaps, and I knew that my route would bring me back this way the next day, but one.

The terrain on the higher ground certainly matched the description of Rough, with little evidence that I was treading where many others had walked before me. Moor grasses and boggy areas gave way to scattered clumps of heather amongst the rocky outcrops and boulders. A steep ascent which involved a bit of a scramble, was followed on the other side by an equally hazardous clamber down; I was indeed glad of my walking poles.

Once safely over the bealach though, I stopped for a welcome break and brew-up. From this vantage, the triumphant ruggedness of the mountain peaks and ridges was clear. Knowing that I'd get the full effect of all this tomorrow, I hoped that the weather would hold to heighten the whole experience. In any event, there were already many photos captured and stored for future use in the camera which I'd always carried ready to hand. What information wasn't on the memory card, was fixed in my mind, waiting to be turned into the right words later.

Finally, dropping down, down, to the small dam at the end of the Loch, there seemed like several good places to pitch the tent on what may have been an old access road for its construction fifty years earlier. Rich in small ground-hugging wildflowers and grasses, it seemed like a perfect spot to camp and from which to explore. Once fed, I set about recording as much of the spirit of place as I could adequately describe, in my notebook.

Next day, I reorganised my rucksack, and left what I wouldn't need for the day in the tent, zipped it up and headed back towards the dam. It stood as a neat little piece of engineering in a very remote location, which seemed to hold back a vast sheet of water as the Loch stretched eastwards for miles, and round behind a mountain or two. Having studied the map, the previous evening, I could see that this structure was the minor one, as the main dam was at the other end of the Loch. Although it all looked a bit unnatural and out of place, it was good to know that the wildness was being captured in some way, and turned into electricity. The compromise for me is that I much preferred this, to the nuclear power that we hadn't a clue how to clean up afterwards. Liz and I had had some great discussions about this.

Just before leaving the dam to head straight up the mountainside to the north, the carcass of a dead sheep lay rotting, stinking in the lee of the concrete; it was a grim reminder of the fragility of life in this vast wildness.

The route for today would take me up and along part of the line on my map, so I wanted to take special note of all that it held the promise of The Spirit and his Seven Signs; this is Nature's holy ground, I let my imagination contemplate. From the summit that I chose as a lunch spot, I could see all of Knoydart, Skye, The Minch and a hint of Lewis and Harris too. A note on my map recorded that this was the westernmost point on the entire seven-hundred and fifty-mile watershed. Ronald had kindly added this statistical fact. While I could see that Scotland's only two fiords are on either side of Knoydart, the lands above the waterheads could almost dip a toe into the brine.

The following day, I'd set off having packed up my camp, and on crossing the dam, had a very steep ascent onto Sgur na Ciche ahead of me. Finding a route, and picking my way cautiously upwards through an almost horizontal maze of crags and outcrops, the going was slow. Each slab presented a new and at first seemingly insurmountable obstacle, where my insignificance was all too real, but each time, a way was found to get around the unclimbable. A new steeply sloping grassy or rocky ledge would conveniently open in front, and point ever upwards. No scope here for stopping to admire the view; that would have to wait. Eventually, though it eased a bit, and there was the opportunity to take in more of the surroundings, so I decided that I'd stop for a break in a while.

Sitting down in the sun, and getting out what I needed for that brew up, I could take in the views once more.

Then I became aware of the sounds of movement nearby; this had me nervous at first, as I'd seen no-one approach; indeed I'd seen nobody for almost two days. Looking over to my left, I could see the figure of a man heading towards me. To my amazement, it was Colin, whom I'd met in Ullapool, all those weeks ago.

"Well, well, fancy meeting you in this out of the way kind of place. How's your great quest going, Andy, isn't it?"

"It's going fine, well more or less. And just fancy meeting you way out here too Colin, but I guess this is more in your patch than it is in mine."

Sitting down beside me on this big reasonably level slab of rock, we chatted for a fair time, caught up on the ups and downs of my venture, and he shared some of the water from my stove for a welcome mug of tea.

"I've been wandering around on Knoydart for a few days, having come in from Glen Shiel in the north of here. Heading out towards Glengarry, I guess. And I'll gladly join you up onto Sgurr na Ciche; then we'll see where we go from there. Glad of the company for a bit."

Our continued ascent varied from more of the very steep to just slightly easier going. Not much opportunity to chat along the way, as each of us picked a route that suited, but it occurred to me, that if this was nature's route along the lands above the waterheads, it had chosen or created a demanding, very uncompromising one. And it's no wonder that this is not the most popular, or tourist way up this otherwise well-loved hill.

At the summit, we found that it suited both of us as a lunch break. We sat there, munched, took in the immensity, and rugged grandeur of the views in every direction, and interrupted this occasionally by commenting on this mountain or that ridge, a loch, or the views out to sea to the west.

"Look there's someone 'way down there, heading in a bit of a hurry towards the dam."

Ae`, he's not hanging about, and that's the way I went, just two days since. Thought we had the place to ourselves Colin, but let's not be precious about it."

"Course not but my, he, well I'm assuming it's a he, is in a hell of a hurry. Strange."

With our lunch break over, photos were taken for the record, bags repacked, and we set off down what may be popularly regarded as the tourist route to the east, beside the remains of an old dyke. I went ahead, as there was no room to walk alongside each other.

About half way down to the bealach, Colin suddenly yelled from behind; "stop Andy, do not move an inch."

This sudden command gave me such a fright that I did stop, stock still. "Christ, what's up mate?"

"Don't turn around Andy, but take one step back up the hill towards me. I'll come down beside you. There's something strung across the path just in front of where you are right now.

Gently does it, Andy, because whatever it is, it shouldn't be there, that's for sure."

Did as instructed, with my heart pounding I managed a very cautious one step back towards Colin, as he came almost alongside me.

"Look, the sun`s catching it now, there`s a wire or something very like it running tight across the path, there, about thigh height. Fuck sake, whatever it is, it should not be there. Hang on Andy, if you can edge to the left a wee bit, I`ve already got my pack off and will take a look."

Steadying myself with my left hand on a jutting rock, I let Colin edge forward to where I`d been. Breathing heavily now, all sorts of thoughts pounded through my mind, not least of them being, `what next`?

"OK, I did a bit of explosives stuff back in the Police days, and am pretty damn sure that where the wire goes into the old dyke on the left, there`s a lump of something that looks very suspicious. The other end of it is securely belayed to that big boulder on the other side. Some unfriendly booby-trap I`d say."

The splendour of the surrounding mountains was eclipsed by the horror of what we`d discovered. Another two steps and we`d almost certainly have been a goner. Oh God, is there no end to what this fucker and his land-owning boss's pedigree will do? They do have it in for me and my harmless purpose. As Colin cautiously inspected what he could see of the device, my despair became very real.

"Here`s what we`ll do Andy. Must get back a safe distance up the hill, get a note of the exact location, and phone the Police. We may be here for a while. Can you work out from the map an exact grid reference for the device, and our location too?" Colin also wanted the name and height of the mountain we were on, and of the bealach, we were aiming for. "Have that info ready, while I phone the Police. They'll summon whatever emergency services seem most appropriate when I tell them what's up."

That done, we made ourselves as comfortable as possible and waited. Didn't have to wait long, though, before a couple of big helicopters drummed their way towards us. Using the bealach lower down as a drop-off, half a dozen military looking characters emerged from each machine, abseiled to the ground. Another smaller helicopter came into sound and sight, as the troops rapidly took control of the entire hillside. We were ordered to re-ascend to the summit and drop a little down the far side.

We were joined shortly by a couple of the military and told to duck down, at which there was a dull thud. "Controlled explosion. Now let's get you safely out of here. But first, did you see anyone else in the area today?"

Happy to let Colin give his account of the hurrying figure we'd seen in the distance, and heading for Loch Quoich, or so it seemed, but that must have been over two, perhaps three hours, ago. A few more questions and the smaller helicopter appeared overhead. In no time at all, we were being winched aboard, and then soaring across hill and glen towards Police Headquarters in Inverness.

The bland appearance of the building seemed in stark contrast to the drama which had just been played out so rapidly in the Rough Bounds. It was only sometime later, that I fully realised what a close shave it'd had been, and my immense relief that it had been a failure. It occurred too that this would up the determination to find the chief perpetrator.

Chapter Twenty-Two

Word must have got around. The next two or three days were a bit of a jumble, with an uncomfortable journey back to Liz`s in Edinburgh, a very rare but welcome visit from my parents, more check-ups, and Police questions. A bottle of fine malt whisky had however been left for me by a couple of former colleagues. Conversations with Ronald continued, and the surprise news of Jamie`s interrogation. In amongst all this, the Police were showing they were very eager to find and arrest the main culprit. The one person who could have contributed most to this was being singularly unhelpful; Jamie was staying tight-lipped and once more at liberty, but under observation, in Aberlady.

It must have been the subsequent shock of it all that left me feeling quite exhausted and unable to function very well. Liz nursed and cared for me with great patience and devotion, at which I did comment that this was under the circumstances, rather more than I deserved of her. She just dismissed this, with a chuckle and idle scoffing.

When others were visiting, she could get out and to press on with the preparations for her exhibition.

Just before I felt ready to head for home to look after myself, and I had to say to myself, give Liz her space and time back, Ronald informed me he`d set up meetings with a couple of people that he was sure I`d want to have involved in the project.

A taxi was summoned to get me there.

Ronald demonstrated his penchant for an egalitarian approach to all, or most things at least when he boldly located the meeting with the television documentary company would be in the popular Story Telling Centre café. They may have been more accustomed to being hosted for such events in The Balmoral, but such was Ronald's pull with these guys, that it seemed fitting, and worked well for him. Having put together a succinct synopsis of all the material we'd assembled on the meaning of The Seven Signs, and the comprehensive evidence to support it, he'd crafted enough of a hook to get them interested, intrigued even, in taking the whole project further.

Not being in any way familiar with these sort of meetings, or the three people that we had with us around the table, I found it best to leave the running to Ronald. Although they seemed to have got wind of the fact that the venture had been quite a hazardous business for me, Ronald very adeptly steered things well away from that, and to hone in on the unique environmental qualities of what we still called The Lands Above the Waterheads. He summarised the origin of the Seven Signs, the meaning of each, and their combined significance for people in Scotland today. The questions flowed to and fro, and somehow, although the television people seemed quite full of themselves, Ronald kept the focus firmly on the core notion of this artery of Nature running for hundreds of miles, from one end of the country to the other.

With more coffees and buns ordered, and the danger of the distraction from other customer's loud conversations, we huddled ever closer together, only drawing back a bit when we unrolled a map of Scotland on the table in the middle of the group.

The discussion eventually moved on to outline their plans for a three instalment documentary series, to be filmed over much of the coming year, and with a view to being broadcast in around the following festive period. Although we just skirted the question of funding, it was evident that money would not be an issue, and they would want my paid involvement in the whole venture.

"We'll want to give it a contemporary political edge too. Think we'll ignore much of the mishaps that seemed to come your way if you don't mind, but will look behind that to draw in the land reform imperatives. This whole scenario will all need to be put into the context of where that's progressed to by the time we produce the series, but it'll pick up on frustrated expectations on the one hand, and the determination by vested interests to hang onto what they've got. That'll draw in the viewers, and set social media buzzing."

Commenting in conclusion, that it would make a fine project, they added that the eco-spiritual side of it was still a bit light, so that would have to be worked up some more.

By the time the meeting broke up, and the television people went their ways, I just looked at Ronald in stunned silence.

Breaking the silence, Ronald brought me out of my dwam, with; "right, that was pretty damned good, wouldn't you say? Now, a wee bit lunch and then the follow-up, which might be a bit more testing. Oh, you look puzzled now, didn't I tell you about the next one?"

"Eh, no you didn't, and that one we've just had would be hard to beat. So, what is it?"

"The trouble with something that stems originally from a Magnum Mysterium, which is really what your Spirit character is or was, is that it's impossible to prove. Don't need to tell you that there's no shortage of sceptics out there, so we need a bit of objective scrutiny of the whole thing; source, quest research and findings, the whole jing-bang. While you were teetering on the edge of oblivion, I took the liberty of enlisting a heavyweight from academia too, what shall we say; review it all? We'd better eat up as Emeritus Professor Anderson is due here in half an hour."

A tall, slim grey-haired lady in smart matching everything and clutching a well-used briefcase strode boldly in the door, and across to where we were eagerly seated.

"Ronald, lovely to see you again, and this must be Andy Borthwick. Very pleased to meet you, and how are you fairing, after all, that's happened to you?"

"Delighted to meet you, Professor Anderson, and I'm getting there, yes, each day gets better, thank you."

"Oh, let's cut the formalities, I'm Jennifer, but I much prefer Jenny."

"We're both most grateful to you for meeting with us Jenny, and glad to see you looking so well. I'll get the coffees ordered up," as Ronald nodded to the waitress.

We seemed to get right down to business without any more ceremony.

"I've studied the very detailed, and thoroughly researched paper that Ronald sent me about a week ago, and it has a rich dimension to it with your experiences and perceptions shining through Andy. It balances the academic, journalistic, and very practical but perceptive experience in the field very well. I guess I'm not here to assess a thesis, so we'll move on to the question: do the theories and arguments stack up against the clues you were given by the eh, Spirit?"

"Yes, we'd appreciate that Jenny. We've been so involved in our ways, that it's not so easy to be entirely objective all the time. From our meeting this morning with the TV documentary folk, we now know that there is indeed going to be a three-part series filmed and put together next year. We need to be very sure of our ground, so your scrutiny, which I know you've already started, will be invaluable. You may want to fire most of your questions at Andy, as you've heard or rather, read, what I have to say?"

Christ almighty, I gasped mentally. No pressure then.

With the coffees on the table, stirred and at the ready, Jenny launched-in.

"Andy, I'm still quite puzzled about The Spirit character, and I'm sure you appreciate why. Is he credible?"

"Yes, I firmly believe he is, in the eco-spiritual sense at least. I've thought long and hard about this and would venture that whatever form he takes, it takes, the spirit of Nature is something we can all if we so wish, become attuned to, and it generously adds a rich new dimension to our lives. We can, of course, ignore it, and dismiss it all as utterly contrary to all things scientific; that is a matter of personal choice. But Nature with all her forces, dimensions, and time-processes is bigger and more profound than we can ever comprehend fully. So why not, a spirit of place and purpose, to draw us into these almost limitless possibilities?"

Ronald was nodding his head in agreement, and while I knew he might have put it differently, he seemed to acknowledge the wisdom in what I was saying.

"Very good, this has the seeds of credibility bound up in it, and your balanced approach to how others might respond to what I would call an act of faith plus, is something that you can work on with confidence."

"Were you in any way a religious man before all this started Andy?"

"No not at all, but this is not about the conventional packaged religion, it's very personal, avoids most of the normal morality obsession about sin, and just draws me into how I can interact with Nature; what I can put in, and what I'll get back. Rather more of the former of these. Hope this makes some sense."

"Yes, I can see how you've formulated a tenet that for you transcends mundane everyday concepts of faith, and pins everything to the natural world around us."

"Ae`, but I don't want to be in any way possessive about it, it's there for everyone."

"Of course, I think you've argued the credibility one well, in so far as it goes."

"I'll want to come back to one element of the first of the seven signs, about the lands above the waterheads, but do have one immediate question, and that is, why do you think it's so important, in simple terms, at least?"

Drawing a deep breath to compose a response, I said, "Well, the answer lies largely in solving the other clues, taken together, they all follow on from it. No one of them exists in isolation from the others. They do make this geographic feature stand out as the most comprehensive and naturally evolved strip of land on this scale left in the entire country. There may be a few places in which it has been sullied, or even corrupted by our activity over time, but it is the least so, on this scale."

"Not a bad argument at all, it comes out well in Ronald`s paper, but you've boiled it down to something factual and dare I say it, inspiring."

"Now, moving on to the third, the one about myriad tops and crags, I think once again Ronald has captured this well by telling us that it is equivalent to well more than four Mount Everests of ascent, and of course descent too. That is singularly impressive. But what do you say of it, Andy?"

"I certainly experienced much of these tops and rocky crags, that's for sure, but it varied enormously between the areas I chose; from the sharp and severe, to the much subtler. What I'd say I was conscious of is that I was always on the higher ground, above that which lay on either side and the unifying link in all of it, this is the line of the watershed. By avoiding talking about things like Munros, it was possible to see how The Spirit somehow embraced the entire line all the way from the south to the north-east."

"Yes, I can see that, but your challenge is still to show conclusively that this myriad collection of tops and crags is quite different or distinct from all of the others."

"Well that's to do with their geographic connectedness; they make absolute sense in that context. And it's my direct experience of these features that give me this confidence."

"Now Ronald, I'm puzzled by all this bog. How can there be so much bog on the higher ground, at the top of the hill, as it were?"

"Ah well, if you'd climbed as many mountains as Andy and I have, you'd know that there is nearly always bog. We are in Scotland, after all. The first thing to say is that of all the clues that we have; the bog one is probably the most topical. There's been more said and written about the importance of bog, both locally and internationally than ever before; it's the in-topic for all sorts of reasons, the most important being how it keeps all that nasty carbon in a safe place Three out of the five ventures that Andy went on, involved bog. And you'll have seen that in my research, I've identified dozens of bogs both big and small on and about the lands above the waterheads, which are designated and protected for some ecological reason or another. Some of them are in the most unlikely of places, like right in the middle of the central belt. The bogs may be only part of the story entrusted to us by The Spirit, but they are, especially by today's standards, central to it. Some are noted as being degraded, and therefore in need of action, while many others are what's called active bog; still living and growing."

"I'm greatly reassured by this, but won't be going climbing any mountains to satisfy myself, I'm afraid, and bog has no aesthetic experiential appeal for me whatever."

"Back to you Andy, for the next one I'd say. All these diverse habitats that are the least cultivated and rather empty, of people, I presume?"

"We do need to do a bit more research to quantify just how empty most of it is, empty of houses and settlement, that is. And there's a lot of this land that has never been settled upon; indeed, could never have been. The areas I visited were entirely uncultivated and probably could never have been either. The word diverse does resonate for me, and I'm sure Ronald's findings will echo that. There's everything from the valley bottom to the mountain top, native woodland to treeless, and all the rest. I only explored a wee bit of it, but anyone wanting to explore more or all of it, would find that no two days would be the same, and I'm not talking about the weather, either."

"No, I didn't think that you were. I'm finding that the picture that you are both creating is well focused, and only the most cynical would have cause or case to dismiss your thesis. Yes, it does, of course, need more work on some parts of it, but it also opens a whole new vista on the potential for eco-research. Which brings me to the one that intrigues me most, where folklore and symbolism touch upon the place of these lands above the waterheads in social history."

"Andy?"

"This is a hard one, as I reckon it cries out for some post-graduate research on the meanings of the names of hill, place and burns. This dimension to it would shine a light on how our ancestors viewed their wee portion of the spine of Scotland. And although I`m no expert, I do know that folklore offers a rich seam of stories, symbolism, and sense of place in the lives of people. None of this should be idly dismissed as fanciful. If The Spirit is correct, and I believe that he is, then we will find that there is much more to the lands above the waterheads than meets the eye. Evasive might be the best way to describe my response here, but there is much-unfinished business. I`m sure you`d agree Ronald."

"Sure would, and it is simply tantalising, crying out to be investigated further."

"Hm, very much as I thought, and although it`s not within my brief for today, I`d be glad to help if I can, as it touches on my areas of expertise, gentlemen. On reflection, I think the issues of symbolism in names and folklore are an essential part of this, so we`ll need to give some thought to how we want to explore and present them. A nice foil to the overly secular world that otherwise surrounds us; that we imagine we feel comfortable in."

"Finally, I`d like to think that you are onto something with the inspiration for the human spirit, but it is, without a doubt, the most difficult clue to pin down."

"It's the one that The Spirit hinted we should aspire too." I cut in. "I think he was desperate to tell me, to instruct me in how I should tune in and switch on. But he knew time was limited, so he could only allude to it, and this he did, with utter confidence and conviction."

"Oh, I can see that. Your big challenge will be to turn it into words and images that people can want to appreciate. For many, it is the most difficult, and dare I say it, awkward. I'd encourage both of you to continue the journey that you've started. It will not all go just as well as you would like it to. You've already discovered who some of your adversaries are, and they are not without influence or purpose. But please persevere, I've enjoyed what you started by calling a scrutiny. Consider that box well and truly ticked, and I look forward to the onward progress of this venture. Some assessments I've done have inevitably ended in tears, but not this one. Now, I must be gone, as I've something to attend to up at the Old Quad. Oh, and if the television folk want a consultant, I'll be more than happy to donate some of my time to the valuable endeavour."

"One final thought Jenny before you go, if I may?"

"No problem, do go on."

"The Spirit called it an artery of inspiration, and we've shown that it's the spine of Scotland regarding geographic place, elevation, environmental integrity, and the likes. Well to my mind, that makes it special, I'd even venture the word unique. But it feeds out in several ways into the wider landscapes beyond. In many places, it's like a seed-bed for native species, and throughout, it's the very source of pure, clean water for land and people. Just a thought, but one that raises the level of resolution to the fundamental importance of what we're looking at."

"No casual aside that one, gents. If we explore all this effectively, we probably have an entirely new take on the Scottish landscape on offer. I couldn't have imagined that happening within my lifetime."

With that, she warmly shook both of us by the hand and following our enthusiastic thanks, left in the same purposeful way that she`d arrived an hour earlier.

"Another coffee?" I ventured.

Waking up in my bed for the first time in several weeks, I felt almost overwhelmed by the unfamiliarity of it. Taking time to remind myself just where I was, the drama and the dangers I`d encountered in the interim, soon welled to the surface. Something very sinister had been stacked up against me in the pursuit of my quest. It was very hard to understand what that might be, but I`d my suspicions, and had every intention of a bit of measured retribution; so, made two phone calls.

A bit of domestic sorting-out needed to be done first, or I`d run the risk of degenerating into a complete scruff. Sorting and cleaning gear is never the most exciting of tasks, but I did pride myself in taking care of all that I`d paid good money for and needed, as it tended to last longer that way. To help me along, I put some music on, loud; a selection of lively traditional Scottish and Irish. `That`ll set the pace; good thing the neighbours will be out`.

First off, all the stuff that needed to go into the washing machine was dispatched accordingly. My selection of fabrics was a bit random, but it usually worked. Next, those items which were damaged beyond repair got consigned to the bin. The items with bullet holes were laid aside, just in case. Finally, that which could be cleaned ready for my kit store was dealt with accordingly. A lot of satisfaction in this, to my surprise, but my wounds were beginning to ache. The appointment that I'd set-up at the health centre was at twelve, so a couple of painkillers were taken, to keep me going. My body had been through the mill, and it knew it. Bruises and lacerations were one thing, but damage by gunshot stood out as being much more severe; this was a rare happening in my book.

On my way to the health centre, I bought what new outdoor clothing that could get in the town, to replace that which I'd lost. It wasn't cheap, so I reckoned my assault had cost a few hundred pounds in clothes alone. The nurse was a bit surprised to see me walking into her clinic bearing a couple of large carrier bags, but at least providing an explanation of the contents and why, also introduced the reason for seeing her. She looked more than a little alarmed as she said "I'm not accustomed to dealing with gunshot wounds here in Peebles. Now damage by broken glass is a bit more commonplace hereabouts, especially just after the weekend. But let's see what needs to be done for you. So where were you first dealt with following your, eh, accident, or was it accidents, plural?

"Oh, this was no accident, it was very deliberate and wanton, and I hope the person who did it gets caught and dealt with in the courts. Shooting people and trying to blow them to bits are serious offences, I believe. However, that aside, it was in the Belford Hospital in Fort William that kindly patched me up. Guess you could phone them for an account of what they dealt with if need be.

"Probably no need. Let's have a look at this first. But hang on, did you say something about being blown up too? This situation is new-territory for me.

"Thankfully that one failed, as we discovered the booby trap just in time. But it has left me very shaken indeed."

Stripping my shirt and fleece off, she gently, but decisively removed the dressings, and examined the wounds.

"OK, I can see what they've done, and the stitching is sound. Did you get a tetanus jag?

"Yes, but I've had a few in my time. What do you think of it, the wounds, I mean?

"Well, it appears as if you've received a long but slicing shot, that has just ripped a fair bit of soft tissue, and not broken any bones, it looks OK. You'll need to get the stitches out in due course, and I'll replace the dressings with a new one now. It's at the top of your arm, so you should be OK to drive, but I'd suggest you take it easy for a wee while. Try and keep the dressing dry, if you can. Come back and see me in a week. Same day and time. Oh, and have you got some painkillers, just in case?"

"Yes, I do. Should be fine. Not accustomed to getting attacked in these potentially deadly ways.

Meeting Angus in the Arts Centre café for lunch, we'd be a good, if brief catch up. By luck he was just back from his latest off-shore shift, so was keen to find out all that had been going on in his absence. There was plenty for me to tell, and recall, so I guess, it was me that did most of the talking. For his part, he was just shocked at what had befallen me.

"I thought you were just off on a nice bit of escaping into the countryside to forget that which should not be mentioned. Thought it was all going to be gentle and involve a bit of walking or cycling, with the most strenuous being a climb or two, perhaps. And here you are going off on some quest, and then getting damned near murdered on several occasions, into the bargain. I'll just stick to mountain biking, if you don't mind, my friend."

"Ae` it's been quite an adventure all right. Tell you what, could I borrow your quad bike, Angus?"

"Course you can, you know where it is, and where the keys are. But what do you want that for?"

"Need to know only for now Angus, but both it and I will be safe. Will tell you when I`m finished with it. But thanks, very grateful."

Most of the food cupboards in my flat were empty, so I called in at the supermarket and got a few supplies to keep me going. On my return, the message received light on my phone was flashing; it was Liz. Calling her back, we`d a brief chat, and she said she`d like to come down for the night and tend my lacerated body once more. "On one condition, though."

"Consider it done, my love." I cut in.

"That's OK then, see you later, probably about six."

"Bye for now."

That was an ultimatum I simply had to meet; to get the flat clean and tidy. Or the parts of it that mattered at least. Swept and dusted, hoovered, and scrubbed. Things that had been lying around were put away, my cleaned outdoor gear was put back in its rightful place, the I emptied the washing machine, and I even hung some of its` contents out on the washing line in the yard. The rest I rather extravagantly put in the tumble drier. Last, and perhaps most important gesture was that I changed the sheets on the bed, and put out fresh towels. Finally, I went around to the florist and got a bunch of spring flowers, to give an impression of freshness. Then I turned the heating on.

Having been away from base for so long, there was a bit of paperwork to be tackled, so the mail was sorted into three piles: recycle, pending, and deal with it now. It was the latter that received my attention, but sadly most of it was in the form of bills to be paid. There was a note from my mother giving the usual news from Newton Stewart, most of which meant little to me, having been away from there for so long. But this had all been superseded by the visit by dad and herself when I was recuperating at Liz`s.

Liz appeared just after I`d finished a rather one-sided phone conversation with mum. As we embraced, I winced yet again; there were parts of me that were still very sensitive indeed.

"Oh, gosh Pandy, I`m so sorry. Is the pain getting any less?"

"Yes, it is thankfully, and don`t worry, saw the nurse earlier, I`m a brave chap. Let`s go out for a bite to eat. All this sitting around has made me hungry."

"You`ve just been sitting around, have you? You promised…"

"Och, I was in such agony this afternoon, which I got my cleaner to give the place a going-over. I think he did an OK job. Go on, check it out if you like."

With a puzzled, but very focused look on her face, Liz went from room to room and scrutinised the place. Coming back, she said "Yes, your cleaner is to be congratulated, very thoughtful to put clean sheets on the bed, and flowers in the vase over there. Thank you, my man," she winked.

Once we'd eaten in the Bistro just along the road, we returned, to see what the night would bring. I was very glad of her company in bed.

Chapter Twenty-Three

Liz had left bright and early the next day, as she'd more urgent work to do for her big exhibition. Thanking her warmly for her visit, we parted with the promise to meet up again, very soon; I'd seen no need to tell her anything about my plans for the day.

Although not normally given to vengeance, such had been the violence visited upon me, that something in me stirred, and I felt there was a score to be settled, or a point made, at the very least.

How I'd managed to convince Jamie to meet me at Glentress near Peebles, ostensibly to try and resolve our differences, was quite an achievement. I'd to dig deep into my powers of persuasion. Perhaps it was his confused state of mind which had made him apparently more amenable. But my suggestion that we go for a walk in the woods somehow met with his approval. This event was no mean achievement given that it was only seven-thirty in the morning when his car drew up beside mine outside the visitor centre. He was dressed, to my surprise, as if he was just about to head off to work in the office.

"Morning Jamie, how's you on this bright and sunny morning?"

"I'm OK Andy, but you're a bit of a swine for getting me to come all the way down here at this early hour. A walk in the woods, you said, there are plenty of woods nearer to home. Anyway, I'm here; you want to talk, I'm listening, let's get going."

"Hang on, let's have a coffee first. Don't know if you've had any breakfast yet, but I've at least brought some coffee and a muesli bar for each of us. Let's sit over at this picnic table."

Ushering him across, I poured two mugs and handed him a healthy-looking snack. Judging by how quickly he got stuck into the coffee and bar, I reckoned that breakfast hadn't been on the agenda for him thus far; mine could wait a bit.

"What is it you want to talk about Andy, I'm all ears?"

"Oh, this and that Jamie. We've had, our differences and things haven't been going well for you and your family of late. I hear that Hermione and the girls are living with her parents right now."

"A temporary situation, I assure you. We were planning some work on the house, so it seemed more sensible to give them space."

`You, lying bastard`, I thought to myself. `From what I hear it's likely to be much more permanent, and the house business is nothing more than a smokescreen`.

Jamie had drained his mug of coffee, and the muesli bar was finished too, so I poured him another generous measure.

"Aren't you having any coffee Pal?"

"Aye` in a minute, I'm just letting it cool a bit first. This mug has some insulation on it."

"Come on, what's all this about Andy Borthwick. I smell a rat."

`It's you that's the rodent`, I said to myself. Good thing he couldn't read my mind.

"Well, we had our wee difference at Aberlady a while back, and things have gone a bit awry for me at least, since then. I'm just wondering."

"Wonder all you like mate; it's no concern of mine."

214

"Ah well, that's not quite how I see it. See, there's a certain sleazy pub in Perth and the company you keep there."

This brought a reaction, but more muted than I'd expected. His brain was slowing.

"Don't know what you're talking about." He slurred. "What the fuck's in this coffee or that bar? You're trying to poison me you bastard." But he was obviously having difficulty focussing on what he was saying, and on how it was coming out.

"Not at all, Jamie. You'll be fine, in the end."

After a brief spell in which he looked around in a confused stupor, trying, struggling to focus on anything, I just hoped I hadn't misjudged the quantity of the stuff with which I'd primed the flask. Slowly and very deliberately, I took a bottle of water out of my bag and drank long and cool.

As he slumped over the table, all the remaining contents of the flask were duly emptied into a bush and some of my water used to flush it out.

Right pal, matey, a dose of your own medicine awaits you.

Thankfully there was still no-one else around, so I swung Jamie onto my shoulders, smarting at the severe pain this caused. He was utterly limp, out for the count, as I carried him over to a shed where Angus kept his quad bike. It had a kind of plastic bread tray strapped on the back, so I dumped Jamie on that. Grabbing the roll of gaffa tape from my bag, his hands were duly bound firmly, if harmlessly together. Then I got a couple of short lengths of rope that were hanging on a hook and tied him to the tray, and to the quad bike frame. He would be going nowhere other than with me.

We roared off out of the shed, still no one around, and away up the tracks that led to the highest point on the cycle trail. Bumpy and noisy the journey may have been, and I wasn't the most skilled of quad bike drivers, but we made it in one piece. Well I was, wasn't so certain about my passenger. Stopping at the viewpoint, and switching the engine off, peace returned, with only the birdsong and sound of the breeze murmuring among the trees for company.

After about half an hour, I was a bit anxious that Jamie hadn't come around yet. He needed to be very alert, or at least mobile, for the next part of this escapade.

By cutting the tape off his wrists, and loosening only slightly, the knots on the ropes, I could see him begin to stir. He slowly emerged from the stupor.

"Where the fuck are we? What have you done to me? Why am I trussed-up like this? Jesus Christ, where is this place? You're an unspeakable shit, you've kidnapped me."

"Language, language Jamie M. Ferguson, you never know the tender gender of these birds that may be listening."

Wrestling with his shackles, he uttered another string of oaths, which I never imagined he'd have even known. But there again, he'd been to a so-called public school; a generic kind of education, perhaps.

"Your public-school education has clearly worked J.M.F, prepared you well for life's adventures."

Releasing the last of the knots in the rope, he immediately fell off the tray onto the ground, almost overturning the quad bike in the process.

"Mind the motor mate; I've only got a loan of this for the day."

"Bugger the motor as you call it, what`s your game? Trying to poison someone is a serious offence you know."

"Well now, is that so?"

"And so`s kidnap. You`ll get locked up for that."

"Now that you mention it, I know a bit more about the inside of a cell than perhaps you do, a lot more. But that might change yet, for you, at least."

"Fuck, I`ve had enough of this caper I want to get back to my car."

Standing up, he immediately fell over and landed in a big muddy puddle.

"Tut, tut, they really should do something about the state of this track. Must mention it to them. You are welcome to get yourself back to your car, right now. The only thing is, you`re at the top of a very long cycle run here in Glentress. I`m going back on this. Pity you didn`t bring your running shoes. You`re a bit overdressed for this exercise, but there`s nothing we can do about that now, is there?"

"Oh, Lord God, you`re not going to abandon me here are you, you, cynical creep."

"No, not exactly abandon you, I will be watching you, but from a distance. Don`t want to really be putting the frighteners on you."

In utter despair, he groaned, "You cunning rat I`m completely lost."

"Oh, it`s quite easy, follow the signs, just like the cyclists do. That should take you back to your car if it`s still there, that is."

Sitting slumped on a boulder, he was sobbing. Somehow, I could muster not one ounce of pity, given the dire deeds he'd had inflicted on me.

"No, before setting off you, sorry spectacle of supposed humanity, I just want to remind you of things like assaulting me and starting a fight at your wife's cousin's wedding party. That was pretty, un-gentlemanly, now wasn't it. Everyone was there to enjoy themselves, and you spoilt it for them. Then, let me see, I seemed to get set on fire in my tent and poisoned. I do wonder how on earth that happened. It certainly wasn't nice and wrecked a good tent of mine. Somewhere in amongst this, I found that my relationship with my dearest Liz, or Elizabeth, your sister-in-law just to remind you, was under threat. Whatever could have caused that, I wonder. You can be assured; I didn't like it."

"Moving on, as it were, someone attempted to drown me, in one of the most remarkable places in Scotland, and having failed in that, they beat me up and locked me in a venison larder beside the carcase of a deer. See, it's all getting quite a lot worse, and there's this nagging question in my mind as to what part you had to play in it all?"

His sobs had turned to groans.

"Oh, there's more, Jamie, much more. Because then I found myself lying on a ledge just over the top of a cliff face; how on earth did that happen, how did I get to be in that very precarious place? Could have killed me. And as if that wasn't enough, I found my car half wrecked, well actually it was Liz's vehicle, and was arrested by the Police, for my troubles. I didn't take to my night in the cells. Does that surprise you?"

"Right now, I'm nursing a gunshot wound in my shoulder, and all sorts of cuts and bruises. All the lovely outdoor clothing that got torn to shreds in that encounter has cost me hundreds of pounds to replace. Money doesn't just fall into my pockets, you know."

What I'm wondering is, what's coming next, but I suspect you know the answer to that. Best not to incriminate yourself, though, so to keep silent would be the best bet for you, at least, well for now, as we'll come back to that."

"If that lot isn't enough, what puzzles me about it is, why? I set off on an utterly harmless quest with the natural world in mind, and somehow, for some perverted reason, you've unleashed a psychopathic killer on me. Not very nice that, I'm sure you'd agree Jamie? The truth of it will all come out, I'm sure, perhaps, when you and your partner are behind bars. If you survive, that is."

"But just to reassure you that I do think about you, I've done a lot of wondering about you. I mean, were you deranged in the first place with your blind motivation to bolster the interests of the old land-owning classes, or did that Major General dude put so much pressure on you that you felt compelled just to abandon any notion of what's right and wrong? Was it you or he that threw the law out of the window? Then there's your side-kick. This is the point at which I do have a tiny grain of sympathy for you, because having unleased his murderous tendencies on me to give me a scare perhaps, I think that you lost control, and found you couldn't reign him in. Well, that's a shame, but here's the consequences of your actions. Get running; I'm right behind you."

The look of shock on Jamie's face, with pleading eyes, cut nothing with me. Whatever this little journey may inflict upon him, it was nothing to what I'd experienced at his behest already.

"Get running, or you'll never get home in time for tea, and as you go, just reflect on what you've inflicted on me. Time for you to be thinking long and hard about the warped social and political values that you and your kind seek to inflict upon the people of Scotland. You need to be reminded pretty forcefully that this is the twenty-first century, not the nineteenth, and that enlightened land reform will prevail whether you lot like it or not."

"Oh, and one final thing, before you hit the trail so to speak, one thing I can never forgive you for is this. Now, I'm not a vindictive sort of person, but you, you, apology for humanity, sought to implicate Liz in this; quite unforgivable. We'll continue to live and love the way we want to, the way that suits us, so there will be no more carping from you on the subject. Right? I demand a confession from you right here and now, and a solemn vow that you'll turn yourself into the Police."

Jamie was almost speechless, perhaps he realised that the game was up, but he did splutter something about it being "too late".

Slowly, he started to run, slip, trip, and slide down the cycle track.

I yelled after him, "Hope no cyclist get you, as they'll be bloody annoyed at you cluttering up their trail, and I think your attire is going to let you down quite a bit. Surprising that, as you've always said you're an outdoorsman. Well, let's be seeing the man in you, now."

The first part of the track was wide enough for the quad bike, so I revved and roared behind him, keeping up the sense of panic. He'd find no way of knowing that I'd no intention of running him over; reckoned that the cycle track and a bit of fear to spur him on would do the business just as well. The oaths continued to waft back over his shoulder, mingled with the yelps of pain and sudden alarm. Colliding with a tree, he fell-over winded and landed in yet more mud. A rock tripped him, ensuring that he could get into no running rhythm. Everything was random, with one succession of traps after another. Branches whipped him in the face and caught his limp drooping hands. At one stage, he lost his footing altogether and tumbled headlong into the forest.

At this point, I`d to leave this track, and take a wider loop on another route suitable for vehicles, but went ahead of him, and waited patiently at another view point. His imminent arrival advertised by yet more yells, groans, foul language, and the sound of blundering through the forest. When he emerged, he slumped on the boulder beside where I was stopped and wept.

"No time for this pathetic performance; you had it all coming to you, you, dangerous clown. Right, reckon you've still got about four miles to do if you stick to the route and don't err from it in any way. Oh, and watch out for the dodgy bridge ahead."

A good vantage point was called for to witness this obstacle. So once again, I took a loop that got me to within a few yards of it. Jamie came careering clumsily down the track towards the bridge, which was preceded by a right-angle bend. He missed his turn and plunged into the very muddy burn. When he emerged, I could see he`d lost a shoe, and so was limping very unevenly. The nice office suit was almost in tatters and his tie at an obscure angle around the back of his neck. `How careless`, I thought, `you've lost your hat`. Blood was running down his forehead and over his eyes. He was a sorry sight.

At least, he`d managed to stick to the track, well almost. But this advantage was shattered, as a group of four, obviously experienced` mountain bikers thundered down the track, and sent him sprawling into the forest once more. Before they disappeared around the next bend, words like "mad bastard", and "danger to humanity" drifted back for Jamie to consider. He couldn't muster any reply.

"Only about a mile now, you're nearly there Jamie. Oh, I'll put your car keys in the ignition for a quick getaway." Taking my final loop, I got back to the rear of the visitor centre, put the quad bike back in its shed, locked up, and hid the keys. Waiting patiently and having a good line of sight for the last couple of hundred yards, I readied myself for whatever might appear. By the time, he did show up I could see he'd lost both shoes, one arm of his jacket, and he'd obviously given up on his tie altogether.

"Nearly there, and you'll be glad to know there's a bottle of good clean water waiting for you on your car seat along with the keys."

This offer was drowned out by another commotion, as two cyclists, who knew they were on the home straight, sent him head over heels into a clump of brambles. He lay there in abject misery, so I went over and hauled him out, by the foot. Standing back, I could see a blurred figure, where mud, blood and clinging vegetation summed up his whole experience.

"One last question Jamie, who is your accomplice?"

"Bugger off"; he moaned.

Chapter Twenty-Four

A week or so later, Liz and I decided that we needed a day together away from Edinburgh, though we reckoned that between us, we'd seen enough of wild spaces and places. She said that there was an exhibition of contemporary nature photography on in the art gallery in Perth that appealed to her, so that set our destination for the day.

Although it had taken some time to get her car repaired after all the damage inflicted upon it in what I now called the Gargunnock Hills incident, we decided that a journey by train was the preferred option. We were both rather absorbed in our thoughts at first. Liz had told me that she'd heard from her dad, that Jamie had been in an accident. Archie had bumped into him a few days earlier, and although the details were all a bit vague, he looked like he'd been dragged through a hedge sideways, and then back again for good measure. There was much for her to ponder over in the current state of her family. While she no longer had an ounce of sympathy for Jamie, she clearly worried about the effect that all that he had done, was having on Hermione and the girls; they did not after all deserve this kind of upset in their lives. Although I'd been right in-the-midst of Jamie's misdeeds, Liz relied on me to help try and keep the whole business in perspective; she depended on me for support through this trauma.

"The exhibition in Perth may give me more ideas, even at this late stage, for how to go about my Fringe event", she broke off from her musings, as the fields of Fife drifted past us.

My thoughts were caught up in all that I'd been through, what I'd discovered, and all that Ronald and I had been able to conclude from this. We were excited by it and looked forward to making something useful of it; creating something to be shared with a much wider public. All the promise of a big television documentary would take the project to undreamt of heights, and I reckoned that if there were any way in which The Spirit could observe, he would be very well pleased.

But I couldn't, try as I might work out where things would lead, with the obvious fact that Jamie and his murderous accomplice had sought to scupper the whole thing and me along with it. There was no getting away from the fact that this was all unfinished business. Only Jamie and I knew that he had had a major dose of his own medicine. Thankfully, I'd to admit, he was still alive, but the Police would be continuing their enquiries, so the matter was far from over. There was no way I could close the chapter, and move on to the next; it all hung over me, still threateningly. The prospect of any court cases and public trials made me shiver with dismay. Yes, I wanted justice, but the price would be a hefty one.

My phone buzzed an incoming text, so I'd take a quick glance at it, and it gave me a real start. It was from Jamie, and just said: "Jock Tweedie, Rannoch Estate". No more than that, but it was enough.

Reaching for Liz's hand, I held it affectionately, and we smiled warmly at each other.

During our walk across the centre of Perth, we still held hands, and silently sought to reassure each other, that all would come right in the end; to affirm all that we are to each other. With a quick stop for a coffee en-route, we found that the silence which had prevailed on the journey up, was broken with talk of photography, the natural world, and as if by contrast; some of the fine buildings we were passing. It was a lively eager conversation.

At the Art Gallery, I let Liz lead the way in our viewing and enjoyment of the fine mix of photographs.

"I never tire of discovering how each photographer has captured an image." She said, almost to herself. "Would I have done the same? But know that I probably wouldn't; my interpretation of landscape and the detail in it would have been very much my own. And that's what makes it all so special for me."

This journey into the creative raised me yet further from my earlier worries, and so, the whole experience was uplifting. Quite unabashed, I kissed Liz fondly when I assumed that no-one would be looking. She responded warmly but clearly wanted to get back to the photographs.

Time passed without comment, but with Liz`s proposal that we go and get a late bite of lunch, I realised that some food would be well received. Suggesting that we go to the Concert Hall café nearby, I added that we`d get a reasonable snack there.

"Sound plan, my Andy man. "

As we were making our way across to this eatery, Liz suddenly grabbed my arm and clearly had restrained herself from shouting out. She just pointed towards two figures making their way along the other side of the open square. Jamie, with all his cuts and bruises, was instantly recognisable, even as he limped awkwardly. His companion, I recognised too, as the person who had tried so hard to shoot me near Rannoch Station. So now I knew.

Standing stock still, I signalled to Liz to keep silent, as together we watched the pair go down Skinnersgate, a small lane leading from the opposite side of the square, and then into the Old Ship Inn near the far end. `Got you, you, murderous pair`, screamed in my brain, as I grabbed my phone and dialled nine-nine-nine.

Although it seemed to take ages to give all the information that the person on the other end of the phone wanted, I just blurted out all the answers that he sought, because I wanted this duo to be well and truly nabbed and locked up.

Around us, people went about their daily comings and goings in this otherwise unremarkable corner of Perth. The very bland back of a big store, a modern glass fronted furniture shop facing us, the more formal side of the Art Gallery and Museum, and further round, my eye caught the green copper roof of the Concert Hall. Small lanes led off at odd angles to other destinations. But we stood rooted to the spot almost sheltering amongst the flowers and shrubs in a long planter that ran alongside the pavement here; the rich colours in stark contrast to the rage welling up within me, when I thought fleetingly of all that this duo had inflicted upon me.

Even before my conversation on the phone came to an end, sirens could be heard, in the distance at first, but getting louder; closer by the second. With the knowledge that a drama was about to unfold right in front of us, I gripped Liz`s hand tightly, and together we waited for the action.

We didn`t have long to wait. The Police must have got the message OK, that two wanted men could be found in a pub just down the lane from the Concert Hall. The sirens wailed and echoed off all the surrounding buildings, as two, three, five or more Police vehicles screeched into the area directly in front of where we had planned to eat. We could see that the far end of Skinnersgate was now blocked simultaneously by yet another vehicle, with a blue flashing light on top. People scattered into the narrow streets, and whatever apparently safe place they could find. The every-day, changed in an instant into a major incident; this Police raid was driven by urgency and menace.

Armed officers poured out of every vehicle door, and instantly it seemed, took possession of the area. From our vantage, we could see that they sealed every possible exit from the short narrow street that the pub occupied. Jamie and his partner in crime had no escape. Within seconds, half dozen gun-fingering uniforms had piled into the pub, and one stayed on guard at the door. Meanwhile, another one scrutinised those people who were still visible or half hidden in doorways. Something instinctive must have drawn her to Liz and me, because before we could even think about it, she demanded to know my name, and Liz`s too. Just as Liz was giving her details, I saw Jamie being unceremoniously hauled out of the pub along with his partner. They were spread-eagled on the pavement and handcuffed by more than one officer kneeling on or beside each of them. This Police meant business.

Ushering us into the safety of the Concert Hall, the Police commandeered an area, to take our statements, record what we had seen, and get to the threads linking this to so many other incidents. By the time I had the chance to look out of the huge windows that overlooked the square, the activity had subsided, some sense of normality was apparently returning, and of Jamie and Jock, there was no sign.

The venue for Liz`s exhibition in the Three Sisters was still being cleared by the previous event`s occupants, as their props moved ever closer to the door, and the chairs stacked ready to go somewhere else in the building. We helped to load a Victorian teacher`s desk, mahogany blackboard easel, mounted map of the empire, and a large abacus onto a trolley. Only then could we survey the empty, if mucky space.

What I could do was a bit limited, as my arm was still painful. Liz and Christine had recruited a couple of friends to help with all this setting up, so I contented myself with wielding a sweeping brush to the floor using just one hand. It worked, well more or less, while all the others went out to the van parked awkwardly at the entrance. They unloaded several large wooden frames which had been assembled and screwed together in Liz`s front garden, a couple of rolls of heavy duty canvas, additional pieces of wood, a toolbox, and crates with lighting and sound equipment. Having got the floor as tidy as possible, I just waited for the exhibition structure and materials to arrive.

The assembly of the display structure had at least been verbally rehearsed beforehand, so everyone seemed to know what they were doing, in what sequence, and with my minor role as go-for. By teatime, the whole array of canvass-clad frames, were in place, secured, and the brace structure to securely attach Liz`s framed and mounted photographs were all in place, just in time for the van driver to return with all the carefully protected landscape pictures. Meanwhile, someone else appeared, with a toolbox of electronic gadgetry, and set the lighting and sound system. These were very much Christine`s area of expertise, and so she worked closely with this electrician. Liz issued instructions about the location for each picture to be placed ready for double-screw fixing. As go-for, I did feel more useful.

With only the next morning to finalise all the arrangements and refine the displays, we were ready for the opening by one o`clock, with only an hour to go before the first visitors would be arriving. Christine switched on the sound and lighting to set the scene. She`d put together a fine collection of music which added mood and atmosphere, with the sounds somehow reflecting the spirit of so many of the photographs. It all seemed to carry the viewer along. She had recorded me reading Liz`s short poems, and I`d followed the instructions to read slowly, with purpose and feeling, and to let my voice rise and fall with the rhythms of the words. Every so often, I could hear my vocal efforts come in quietly at first, flow, and then fade, for the next musical piece; hopefully, my self-consciousness wasn't too obvious.

As the final attention to detail before the opening went on around me, I became emotional at the thought of the contrast between the chaos of all I`d been through, the revelation of great discoveries made, and the apparently managed calm of this carefully structured event. Packing in that job had certainly opened-up some unimagined events; the consequences were entirely unpredictable. But I knew that Ronald and I had unravelled the meaning of the Seven Signs, and carried forward the Quest, which The Spirit had entrusted to me

Just after two o`clock, the small but obviously eager crowd was hushed by a sign from Christine. They listened intently as a colleague of Liz`s made a short speech, and commented upon the photo-environmental treat that awaited those who visited this very special exhibition. After the applause, Liz and I stood back in the shadows, waiting, and watching.

Visitors were handed glasses of wine and pointed towards the nibbles on a table at the side of the entrance. Slowly, they moved around the exhibition, soaking up the natural landscapes on display accompanied by the rise and fall of music and my sonorous voice. It all seemed to auger well, as the light buzz of comment and conversation drifted our way. Occasionally, a finger pointed to this frame or that, with muffled exclamations of apparent delight. Some guests spoke to us, to Liz, scribbled a few notes for future reference; by a reviewer, perhaps, hopefully.

Squeezing Liz's hand once more, and glancing her way, I could see tears trickling down her cheeks – tears of joy and relief that this had all come to pass.

Chapter Twenty-Five

The gardens at Spurryhillock had long been abandoned to neglect and Nature's ways, with only a flagstone terrace running around three sides. A small rough lawn clung-on cautiously to the south, with vehicles kept in their place around the door on the opposite side. Built with coursed local stone, it stood two storeys with attic windows above. Archie had had all the external woodwork re-painted to freshen it all up, in readiness. The family had taken up residence for the summer holidays throughout August. Archie and Marissa arrived first to open-up the house, with Hermione and the girls following a week later. Other cousins, relatives and friends dropped in for a few days in turn, and by the time Liz and I arrived for the last week, Spurryhillock had a lived-in welcoming atmosphere. A curl of smoke from one of the chimneys signalled that a log fire would as ever, be burning in the dining room hearth with no concession to the summer season.

On the first evening, before dinner, Archie's suggested to me that we go for a wee walk with the dogs 'to work up an appetite'. Liz nodded her full consent to being left with the other women and girls. The favourite route for this stroll went, up past the farm buildings, with the remains of the old house languishing in the woods down to the left, through a couple of fields with beef cattle grazing apparently at ease, and then onto the small hill topped with an ancient cairn. Fine views out to sea and a carpet of late wildflowers completed the scene.

"Will Jamie's absence make for any awkwardness, Archie?

"No, not really, he's in a secure place pending investigation and reports. You'll probably know more about that process than I do Andy. It may be that there will be nothing conclusive until his accomplice comes to trial, as his deeds are without a doubt the more serious. The girls and Hermione are, in truth, the happier and more at peace without Jamie. We'll just continue to enjoy our summer holidays. Marissa and I are delighted that Elizabeth and yourself are here, that her exhibition was such an acclaimed success, and you seem to have completed much of your venture without any more harm coming to you."

"Yes, I'm so glad this is how you see it all Archie, and we're very glad we could make it here. There's one thing I need to say to you, by way of a confession perhaps. It'll bug me if I don't try and deal with this."

"Go on Andy; I'm always glad to listen."

"Well, somewhat to my dismay, I found that the violence that I experienced, seemed to bring out a violent streak in myself; one that I didn't know I had."

Gazing idly out towards the coast, I could see that Archie was, in fact, taking in what I was saying.

"Towards the end of the whole business, although I, we, got everything we wanted regarding the Seven Signs, discovered all that is bound up in them, and have a television series coming up in the next eighteen months, I found I'd compromised my standards by giving Jamie a dose of his own medicine. Looking back, I'm not proud of it, but do take responsibility for it."

Archie turned towards me and ventured quite casually; "you'll be talking about his little experience in some forest near Peebles, I imagine?"

"Why, yes, I am, how on earth did you know about that?"

Greatly relieved that he already knew at least something of it, I relaxed a bit.

"Oh, I visited Jamie myself where he is currently locked up. He is my son-in-law after all. No one else knows about this, so you might like to help keep it that way. We had a good long chat, and amongst it all, he told me a bit about it. Did say he was rather surprised that you had such an apparently angry streak in you, but acknowledged that he had what he got, or something very like it coming to him, so he`s not bitter. What you did, was somewhat beyond the pale, but just to reassure you, I don't bear you any ill-will for it either, Andy. I don`t imagine that Elizabeth knows anything about this, would that be so."

"No, haven`t had the courage to tell her yet."

"Well, if I may say so, I think you should. I`ve arranged a night for the two of you in a fancy hotel not too far away, and you can pick your moment then. I`ll tell the others, and no doubt will be able to find a way to do this that causes no hurt. You can now relax Andy."

"Thank you; this is indeed generous of you Archie."

"Nae bother, as I believe they say in some circles."

The week ran its course in a convivial spirit. Archie had been true to his word, and although there were some initial quizzical looks, I soon realised that present family affections seemed untarnished.

Liz was showing uncharacteristic nervous excitement at dinner on the final evening. It was Archie who was the first to pick up on this when he commented; "you look like the cat that stole the cream Liz, you just can`t sit still, and your face is alight. Are you OK, anything you`d like to share with us?"

All eyes in the dining room of Spurryhillock turned towards Liz, who blushed with the sudden attention. The fire in the hearth crackled, and the warm flickering light reflected eagerly it seemed, off oak, mirror, and wine glass alike.

"Well, I've some very good news to share."

At which I could see Marissa lean forward eagerly, to catch the gem she clearly anticipated. "No, not that mummy, sorry. But I got an email today from someone who'd visited my exhibition and must have been speaking to you too Andy. It's from an American Arts Organisation that wants to commission me to work on a solo photo project to capture Seven Signs and The Spirit of the Watershed, as they called it. They want me to record and present something of the unique qualities bound up in it all, with its wider and very contemporary potential. They also want a book or pamphlet to go along with it. I've accepted of course. Reckon I'll need your help with this life-changer, Andy; it's like the sleeping giant has just been woken from its very long slumber."

Everyone seemed speechless at first, but I broke the trance, by standing up and walking around the table to give her a big affectionate and unhurried embrace. "Congratulations my love, I'm thrilled to hear this fantastic news."